MARK BLACKLOCK was born in Sunderland in 1974. *I'm Jack* is his first novel.

More praise for *I'm Jack*:

'Less a novel and more an assault on the senses, *I'm Jack* cleverly uses intertextual trickery and deft Mackem parlance to create a portrait of a man obsessed. It is a forensic montage, a frenzied confessional and a stark commentary on the effects of public notoriety. Moving, haunted and necessary' Benjamin Myers, author of *Pig Iron*

'Compelling, troubling, fascinating, a delight to read. It is a sublime anti-novel and a brilliantly original intervention into a most peculiar episode of recent history' James Miller, author of *Lost Boys*

'Absorbing and fascinating. Using multi-layered storytelling, a deep personal knowledge of Sunderland past, present and legend in a believable and hard-hitting blend of fact and imagination, it paints a genuinely disturbing vision of an obsessive, calculating and ultimately self-destructive personality' Bryan Talbot, author of *Dotter of Her Father's Eyes*

I'm Jack

Mark Blacklock

GRANTA

spottys hole broken head little patterns mixed up in theh all these berrels and whirlpools spinnin tugetha all these slicks driftin on thsufuss like petrol or diesel greeny-bluey sheen on top uv the brown churn all flowin out tu sea all gettin washed down the wiah unspoolin in the watta all the guts uv it innards out all the fish guts on the harbar the herrin guts the wifies guttin them brown loops uv it the wyrms wunda iv thes lampreys theh used tu eat them in auden days queeah-lookin things what the lambton wyrm was the lambton lamprey the fust thing he fished out not what it becum not the whoppa started eatin cows udders ahve nay idea that lad didnt know a lamprey when he saw wun he wuz just a bairn cum heah me little jacky now ahve smoked me baccy lets hev a bit uv cracky till the boat cums in shud uv ganti church thats why it went wrong furim deed sumthen he shudunt uv buggered off in the croosayuds thats more church than enywand want but it dusent work it always cums back evry-thin ye dee graws down the bottom uv the well gets bigga starts eatin sheeps and lams and carvs iv yev caught sumthen yeh cun hoy it back iv yeh like but it stays caught wu yoosti gan fishin down south hylton walk under the A19 me dad wuz part uv a fire crew durin the war theh wuh fillin up on the south hylton side on the causeway got mortal left the enjin theh it slipped back in the watta thall got shit fu that fu yurs afta we yoosti gan afta sprats an poddlas an flatties hed a sharp stick a dabba sometimes yed get a safety pin or sumthen bend it inta heuk tie it onti a bit uv string put a wyrm on the end not a proper bait wyrm lugwyrm or raggy I know that now not a mealywyrm a slowwyrm a earthwyrm that waz daft wazunt it but we didnt know eitha me an Stanley didnt know the difference why shud wu? No wun telt us a wyrms a wyrm thought that wyrms joined back tugetha iv you cut them intu bits used tu cut them intu bits the hole time put them in a jar wait fu them tu get hole again it nevva happened the two halves just curled up tight then died that wuz cruel that mind but it wuz from the story thats why wu thought that because Johnny Lambton has tu let the bits uv the wyrm wash away so it dusent join back tugetha nevva caught nowt only eels once or twice mudhoppas bottom-feedas well yeh wudnt with that geah wud yeh wudnt catch a trout or onythin even iv thu wuz fishes in theh probably wusent the rivers bowkin evrywun dumpin theh guts in it evrythen in it from bishop auckland down from stanhup down the weah the browney all the little spewin streams runnin down the denes bet it wuz clean back in the auden days Vikens and that theh wuz loads uv that rape and massacre she and me when we met it wuz mordor just natterin in the pub would yeh like a drink pet uv course mines a babycham aw aye classy not really ah just like the fizz it tastes like shite really though dusent it ahd rather hev a pint uv Macewans tu be honest drink what yeh like pet divent dee onythin on mah count ahm buyin gan on then a lager wud be lush got stuck in had a cackul the dole is my shepherd I shall not work woke up next mornin at hers neither uv wu knew how just washed up theh tide went out and theh wu wur the two uv wu in hur bed meant tu be she wuz all hot under the cuvvas gizza kiss with breath like mine hairy breath wu hed a giggul wu wur still paraletic hed a

cuppa two shugas Bessys hole all these holes went as far
as chester le street chartershoff bridge mebby that wuz it
near the lion park theh shuttin that down now the fairytale
museum all that in the cassul thes them big wavy slides and
monkeypuzzle trees thats what the kids like me mam says he
wuz in the paypas lord lambton got caught out by the paypas
they called him the lambton wyrm whisht lads no wun sez
that do theh not heah mebby in scotland or New cassul but
not heah had yer gobs ahll tell youse all an aaful story he
wuz screwin tarts me mam says got what he dusurved them
posh lords an that livin the high life in lundun no surprise
really me mam says he wuz smokin dope too two wimun in
his bed wun uv the lads what most people thought probably
ahll never be caught with two wimun whores or otherwise
wun wud be nice the rail bridge is just theh ah wud've liked
tu see trains gannin awa the top uv the queen alexandra a
gull sumthin still flappin in its beak sum fish or wyrm white
spillin from yuh breath neara than the clouds faint in the
darkness a name namin nun the knucka hole the dust disused
railway aud minin track black track along the valley tu
Pittntun Tow Law Copt Hill Mad Max it wuz good that tress-
pass Houghtun East Raintun coastal winds the sky above
Seaham scabs on theh backs from carryin sacks the indus-
trial estate in Doxfud Park Seafuth Road teluvishun static
the coast silent Peterlee Hutton Henry fetid and fusty unused
mind thehs a man lives on the beach near Easinton colliery
jammer says or mebby its dawdon wind rips round sick
orange from the point sum kaynd uv lights grey sea coal the
rivva flows out tu sea and so du we evrywuns got sea in them
sumwheh that statue uv Jack Crawfud in Mowbray park
local sailor hero proudest son he wuz mortal though thats
wad theh reckun Jack Crawfud canny lad when he wuz

blotto ah like a drop mesel when ah can get it sly and thou my bonny bairn will likt as well as I Bobby Shafturs gon tu sea thinkin sumwun elses thoughts ahm thutha the days go on and on they don't end cars gannin past sprayin the rain up the pavement but it dusent reach us ahm on the edge ahm that far away ahm just a thicka bitta darkness a mizzul in the murk no wuns stopped this lad walkin past

Excuse me son. Are you alreet up theh?

Aye, ah'm canny.

You wanna be careful or you might fall. Its a long way doon, that.

Aye, ah knaa. I just like lookin at the watta.

You sure? Only its hoyin it doon.

Aye, this coats dead dry. Thanks.

Nay bother. Gan canny, like. Divvent dee onythin daft.

Ah, nah, its nothin like that. Ahll bet its cold in theh.

Three or four degrees tops. Yeh'd last five minutes. Alreet then son. Night then.

Aye Goodnight

wur down at the beach in seaham and davver says this is the beach out uv that fillum which wun that wun with michael caine when the gangster cums up tu New cassul get carter ah always think uv gus carter the bookies when theh says that aye that wun whats it deein heah its meant tu be New cassul that's fillums fu yeh torrens uv rain the like tang uv the rust ahm God's lonely man ahm just a little fishy on a little dishy ahm a poor aud shifta now wad gud can swearin dee ah am a rock ahm an ayeland it all flows through me Stanley cum back from catterick with a tape yev got tu see this john lad proppa video nasty what like drilla killa yull see all scratchy the picture all lines on it copy uv a copy says Stanley from America mickey got it off a marine theh wuz no sound no actin just doctas in coats cuttin up bodies all diffrunt cullas blue green black not black like tar black like soil skin like thick paypa like a rainbow red and yella and blue and green theh wuz this bit with this drop uv liquid just watchin this drop the cullas a body goes ah hope they don't fish us out ah dont want tu be blue or grey ahd rather float away with the fishes ah don't want them cuttin us up theyd find nowt thehs nuthin tu see ahm empty inside the worst bit wuz the start uv each wun thehd cut across the forehed behind the eeas peel back the fayuss like yu roll up a jumpa or pull off tights that wuz worsen the guts all the butchers slops yexpect that seen stuff like that in zombie fillums dawn uv the dead wheh theh chew that lads head off but the fayuss just took away like that the video ett this tayp up Stanley says ballucks thats mickeys tayp ah said thats dun now that Stanley yeh cannat fix it all the thick tayp chewed up in the geahs uv the machine you cannat wind it back in theh difficult tu fix videos aant theh? theh dont wind back it all gets folded in ontitself gets these lines across not smooth onymore won't play proppa gets chewed each time once yev seen it it stays in yhead foldin fayusses yeh cannat go back tu before thes things like that things yeh cannat think back tu before once yev thought them thoughts that stay they cum tu yeh in the mornin when ye wake up and yeh cun push them down but theh cum back cum swirlin back cannat lock them out things yeh think thats why yeh drink that wet carpet ripped up bits uv carpet that have been left outside all soft and mushy cardboards the worst it rips woodlice undaneath loads uv them and wyrms peelin up the carpet lookin beneath damp patches on the walls rust on the bridge bad lads from Hendon gannin down tu Lundun in a transit puttin the frightnas on sum cockney gangstas seein isunt what *people suppose it is the slowwyrms way rot and decay soil slugs leaves mulch wyrms sea caked sand imprints uv rubber boots soles a spoor washed clean away in brown spoil scourin wind shrillin sour breath empty shells stings yeh fayuss wiv pins uv ice rain put a hand up tu wipe your cheek wunda iv thes been many jumpas off uv this bridge she must fetch up sumwheh iv it wuz only in hell loads uv hells clouds piled up like giant rocks rise and dip in the ground swell don't want tu go inside again black spit and lung bill went tu visit jammer in durham jail left his stuff in the visitas centre and hed thirty pound nicked out his wallet white-tops foldin in on themselves and fallin cannatt see out tu sea but thehs mooahd tankas like ghosts at the edges squeeze my knees tight in me chest watch the sky wind rushin breathin mind spinnin blood pumpin in me temples air burnin me lungs ah see the dark itself like stuff will ah swalla great gobfuls uv salt watta limbs dead weight at the ends uv strings like a puppet labberin in the watta drunin tears streamin down me fayuss a mould uv truth shite on me hands disinfectant no good the bleach stings me skin love is so sore its only because uv thems not theh yeh know who ah am evrythin ye think cums from the past thats whats real but it dusent join up onymore ah dont join up its a cheat the sky has hope and mystry the sea washes away the sky is full uv questions the sea is ansas thurth is flat no hope uv goin back hell in my heart its eezia tu fall than tu rememba George*

PE8133 HMP Armley, Leeds, 27th October 2005

Dear George,

Lord it feels strange to write to you again after all these years. I know it would of had you in fits George to think that I was writing now from inside Its what you would of wanted. You would probably wonder why me why am I writing to you again, The answer to that George is pretty simple There is no one else who would understand. Its you or no one George And I want to tell someone because I couldn't tell them in the police station George even if Id wanted Paul Hamilos advised very strongly against it said Id be inside for longer if I said anything except what he told me and whatever people may think I dont want to be inside for any longer than I have to.

Well I suppose I should begin by explaining that I did get caught. You know I didn't kill those girls George cause after they took you off the case they found peter sutcliffe didn't they. That was a lucky accident cause it never looked much like you'd find him without one and you may say that was because of me. Ill be honest I didn't think Id get caught now not after so long and not after theyd got peter Sutcliffe but you lot are like elephants. Id forgot truth be told but your lot hadn't. It was nearly thirty year ago George can you believe that.

I came round in a cell and I did'n't know where I was. I can tell you now thats a grim experience. I'd be lying if I said it had never happened before but it has been a long time and police cells don't hold good memories for me. I dont suppose you ever came round in a cell George although I know that you liked a drink you might have just to have a little kip. Its not a place to wake up. First you think why then you think how then you think Lord not me. they took me to Gateshead first but I've no idea about that "no recollection". Then they drove me down to Wakefield in a traffic car flashing lights and the works. I would of loved that when I was a kid but that's a blur and all just motorway lights flying past my head.

I didn't know where I was and they had to tell me. You're in Wakefield John. You've been arrested. What for For questioning in connection with a tape and some letters sent to police in the 1970s.

They had a police surgeon come in and give me the once over Took my temperature and blood pressure asked me to say Aah and checked my pulse. He seemed happy enough He asked if I would object to a blood sample and a saliva sample. I said theres not much blood in there these days but youre welcome to try. My mouth was a bit dry so he asked if I wanted anything to drink I said I suppose a can of ciders out the question. Then they had a headshrinker come and talk to me. This feller comes in and introduces himself. My name's Dr Dennis Duncan I'm a consultant at Leeds Infirmary I knew it was serious then George When you lot look after people you know they've done something bad.

We had a natter me and this feller. He wasn't so bad. He asked if I'd been treated okay asked if I had any concerns about what was happening to me. He asked if I had a history of mental health issues I said no but I asked if I could borrow his shoelaces He didn't think it was funny. He asked about the booze George I smelt like a brewery. He didn't think I was in too poor a shape give them the go-ahead anyway because next thing I was talking to the duty solicitor who told me the coppers wanted to interview me. This lawyer Paul Hamilos he was a canny lad George. Had my best interest at heart. He said he didn't know anything beyond what the police had told him that I'd been arrested on suspicion of connection with the Yorkshire Ripper hoax tape and letters. He said I had a right to silence if that's what I wanted and advised I shouldn't say anything until we knew more. I said I was fine with that and we went over to the interview room.

Gavin Weale was there with another copper DI Partington an appropriate adult a woman sat in the corner called Katherine. The solicitor says I can tell you this is John Samuel Humble and thats about it because hes not going to talk to you. That must make the police very jolly George when people do that.

Well I wasn't going to spill my guts straightaway George not after thirty year. I've been arrested plenty times before its never nice but you get better at it. I did what we'd discussed me and Paul. I had nothing to say so I said nothing. Gavin Weale kept asking me questions George but I didn't say anything if he asked us a yes or no question I shook or nodded my head but if he asked me where did you go to school I did nowt.

He told me I was being filmed by two cameras. Well I knew I was important George but two cameras. He asked about my family. He kept asking do you understand what's going on he said now was the time to talk about it. He asked again and again and again what I knew about the ripper inquiry and each time I shook my head. are you sure. are you sure there's nothing you want to get off your chest. he leant in close George all confidential like it was just me and him down the pub not me and him and the other three people saying nothing and the two cameras and lord knows how many people watching on them. George I know you would want to be in that interview and I feel I owe you that. Maybe you were in there George a ghost in the machine in the cameras perhaps. But just in case I will show you all the words.

When they gave me my next break after five o'clock Paul came in to my cell and told me that they had DNA evidence. He said it did not mean that they had me bang to rights it just meant that they thought they had it. He said he advised me to maintain my silence in the interviews He said there might be any number of things wrong with their evidence and that it might not amount to anything in court.

I'll be completely honest George I felt sick as a dog. It was the longest I'd gone without a drink for years. They gave me water and offered me tea but my hands were shaking George the DTs did you ever get those. I wanted to puke but then after that came something else It just felt like something had gone something heavy weighing me down I suppose I was feeling a bit lightheaded. I told Paul I was done. He said I strongly advise this and that but I said I'd made up my mind.

When we went back in to the interview room sometime after seven I spoke to Gavin Weale I gave him my name and address myself and when he asked about the letters I said Aye I did send it. The rest is history now George what I told Gavin Weale. It's all there on the film.

I told him that I regretted it George. That I didn't know anymore why Id done it how sorry I felt for the lasses that got killed after. I did feel sorry George I felt Like I might aswell have killed them myself. Id never thought that youd send the cavalry to Sunderland didn't occur to me. I thought I was doing you a favour. I thought you were just messing about

Couldn't give a toss because they were prostitutes. And I was right wasn't I. I did help Did intensify the search. You looked a lot harder after my letters. Not really my fault if you looked in the wrong place. Well that's a lot for one day Ill write again soon George.

Yours sincerely your biggest admirer
Jack the Ripper

West Yorkshire Police
Record of interview with John Samuel Humble at
Wood Street Police Station, Wakefield, 19th October 2005
Interview commencing 16.32

DS Gavin Weale: Please could you give me your name, your address and your date of birth?

Paul Hamilos: I can tell you this is John Samuel Humble. I am telling you who he is because Mr Humble has indicated to me that he is not going to say anything at this stage. His address is ████████ Road Sunderland and his date of birth is the eighth of January 1956. I have advised Mr Humble not to make any comment at this time because there has been no disclosure with regards to any evidence that has linked him to this inquiry.

DS Gavin Weale: Thank you Mr Hamilos. John, are you still happy with that?

[Mr Humble nods]

DS Gavin Weale: So to confirm, do you intend on answering any questions over the course of this interview?

[Mr Humble shakes head]

DS Gavin Weale: Do you understand that a record of this interview, giving details of all the questions asked, will be provided to the court in the event of a trial? Do you understand that?

[Mr Humble nods]

DS Gavin Weale: John, I would like to make you aware that this interview is being recorded by two different cameras which are located on the wall there and there. A video recording of this interview will therefore also be available to the court. Do you understand?

[Mr Humble nods]

DS Gavin Weale: John, this interview is about finding out the truth of what happened and to give you an opportunity to give your explanation. We will approach this interview with an open mind but we will check what you say. There is no rush so consider the answers that you intend to give, but John, I expect you to tell the truth. Do you understand?

[Mr Humble nods]

DS Gavin Weale: We are investigating the sending of letters and tapes in relation to the Yorkshire Ripper murders in 1978 and 1979. Could you tell me everything you know about that, John? I would like to know every detail. Please take your time.

DS Gavin Weale: This is your opportunity to tell the truth. Our inquiries suggest you are responsible for sending the letters – explain to me everything you know about that, John.

DS Gavin Weale: This is your opportunity to tell me your version of events, your side of the story. What can you tell me about it, John?

DS Gavin Weale: Okay John, I just want to recap. You have indicated that you intend not to give any answers to any questions. You understand that a transcript of this interview will be provided to the court as evidence in the event of a trial, so a jury will see a record of all the questions you have chosen not to answer. You have also acknowledged that you know that this interview is being recorded. You understand that we want to hear your version of events, but you have declined so far to give us any such statement. Is that an accurate summation of our interview so far, John?

[Mr Humble nods]

DS Gavin Weale: When were you born, John?

DS Gavin Weale: Were you born on the eighth of January 1956?

[Mr Humble nods]

DS Gavin Weale: Where were you born?

DS Gavin Weale: Are you from Sunderland?

[Mr Humble nods]

DS Gavin Weale: Are you from Castletown?

[Mr Humble nods]

DS Gavin Weale: Can you tell me exactly which part of Castletown you are from?

[Mr Humble shakes head]

DS Gavin Weale: Can you tell me the names of any of your brothers or sisters?

[Mr Humble shakes head]

DS Gavin Weale: Have you got a brother?

[Mr Humble nods]

DS Gavin Weale: Have you got a sister?

[Mr Humble nods]

DS Gavin Weale: Are your parents still alive?

[Mr Humble shakes head]

DS Gavin Weale: Which school did you go to?

DS Gavin Weale: Did you go to a primary school?

[Mr Humble nods]

DS Gavin Weale: Did you go to a high school?

DS Gavin Weale: Did you go to a comprehensive school?

DS Gavin Weale: Did you go to a school after junior school?

[Mr Humble nods]

DS Gavin Weale: What is the name of that school?

DS Gavin Weale: I'd like you to tell me about what you did after school. Will you tell me about that please, John?

[Mr Humble shakes head]

DS Gavin Weale: Did you remain in Sunderland with your employment?

DS Gavin Weale: Did your work keep you in Sunderland?

[Mr Humble shakes head]

DS Gavin Weale: Will you give me the place of employment you worked outside Sunderland?

[Mr Humble shakes head]

DS Gavin Weale: This is your opportunity to give me these details. It will be in your best interests to communicate this information and give your side of the story. What is the name of your doctor?

DS Gavin Weale: Are you registed at a doctor's surgery? Do you have a doctor?

[Mr Humble shakes head]

DS Gavin Weale: What is your blood group?

DS Gavin Weale: Do you know your blood group?

[Mr Humble shakes head]

DS Gavin Weale: Do you have any medical problems we should be aware of?

[Mr Humble shakes head]

DS Gavin Weale: Are you in a relationship at the present time?

[Mr Humble shakes head]

DS Gavin Weale: Have you been in a relationship recently?

[Mr Humble shakes head]

DS Gavin Weale: In the past ten years?

[Mr Humble nods]

DS Gavin Weale: Have you been married?

[Mr Humble nods]

DS Gavin Weale: Could you tell me the name of your wife?

[Mr Humble shakes head]

DS Gavin Weale: Where were you in 1978 and 1979?

DS Gavin Weale: Were you in Sunderland in those years?

[Mr Humble nods]

DS Gavin Weale: Who were your associates at that time?

DS Gavin Weale: Who was your employer?

DS Gavin Weale: Were you employed?

DS Gavin Weale: Have you ever suffered from a speech impediment?

[Mr Humble nods]

[Mr Humble shakes head]

[Mr Humble nods]

[Mr Humble shakes head]

DS Gavin Weale: Which is it, John? You look confused. It's a simple question.

DS Gavin Weale: I am trying to find out more about you, John. I want to know who John Samuel Humble is, what sort of person he is. Each of these questions is asked to give you the opportunity to talk about yourself, if at any stage you decide to change your mind.

DS Gavin Weale: Do you understand?

[Mr Humble nods]

DS Gavin Weale: I'd like you tell me everything you know about the Yorkshire Ripper inquiry.

DS Gavin Weale: Do you know about the Yorkshire Ripper inquiry?

[Mr Humble shakes head]

DS Gavin Weale: Are you sure you don't know anything about the Yorkshire Ripper inquiry?

DS Gavin Weale: Whatever you can tell me about it, John, tell me. If you are involved with these letters, John, surely something must be on your mind and has been on your mind for a long, long time. This is the opportunity, John, while we are here to deal with it.

[Mr Humble shakes head]

DS Gavin Weale: I think it is, John. Have you heard about the Yorkshire Ripper inquiry?

[Mr Humble nods]

DS Gavin Weale: So you do know about the Yorkshire Ripper inquiry?

[Mr Humble nods]

DS Gavin Weale: The Yorkshire Ripper involved Peter Sutcliffe; it involved his behaviour in the late 1970s and early 1980s when he killed several women. What was your interest in that inquiry, John?

[Mr Humble shakes head]

DS Gavin Weale: Do you know about these letters, John?

DS Gavin Weale: Have you sent these letters, John?

DS Gavin Weale: If you are involved with this, surely this must have been on your mind for a long, long time. Surely this is the opportunity, John, while we are here to deal with it.

[Mr Humble shakes head]

DS Gavin Weale: I think it is, John. I am looking for an account, what we are seeking is an account.

[Mr Humble shakes head]

DS Gavin Weale: You have the opportunity to answer these questions and to talk to me about this.

DS Gavin Weale: Let's take a break there, John. The time now is 16.55. Would you like a drink of water?

PE8133 HMP Armley, Leeds, 30th October 2005

Dear George,

This is not a nice place George. Medomsley was grim but this is different more chaos. Theres lads coming and going all the time not much time out of cells. Two in a cell my mates Howie from Skipton. Says he was a farm labourer says he didn't do it I didn't ask what it was but he told us anyway got in a fight and smashed this kids head in, Im not surprised hes a big man George. I told him that and he seemed happy enough.

Cells cold at night shrieking all hours of night and day. Lads crying for their mams Lads yelling to them to shut up Threatening violence. Guards telling them lads to put a sock in it. Oh its a lot of noise George cant sleep very easy but I suppose Ill get used to it.

I was rotten sick when I first got here doctor said it would be three days after my last drink and he was right. Hed give me some tablets diazepams and campral and they helped with the shaking but not the horrors the feelings like I should not have been born like my skin was dead like my hair all dried out. I could not look in the mirror George I could not bear to see my face the yellow teeth the bones beneath. At night I could not sleep but I saw things I saw rats George big black rats crawling over my sheets in the night hiding in the shadows scritch scratch like a sea of them like a river through the cell foul things, We had mice at home got in the cupboards thats why we got the cats first time to keep the mice down but nothing like this fat wet furry black things it was more like the moving than the shape of them. My heart was bursting out my chest George I rang the bell for help three times on the first night each time one of the warders came and turned the lights on showed us there was nothing there calmed us down and when it went dark they come back again crawling all over each other all over the floor trying to get up the bed I waited as long as could thinking it was all in my head but when the weird smells come George like sewage smells I rang the bell again screaming blue murder. the warders said they couldn't smell anything but it was real to me. During the day shakes come back and feelings like the world is going to end like all happiness was gone from the world I was sicksicksick the doctor was sent to my cell said this was the drink too but that my world has changed because my drinking has stopped at the same time as my arrest so depression is almost inevitable they will keep a close eye. Next night insects flies a wall of flies all shifty squashy slick like bluebottles you know them horrid fat bastards all hairy and shiny green and blue ninety-nine brown bottles smeared up a wall. I could feel them crawling on us George on my belly my legs up my arse God George I didn't know the drink could do this I bet you didn't either. They give us a shot that second night but I still see the odd one George the odd fly here or there where they shouldn't be in my food in my hair. Its got better now George doctor says the tablets are working better now says Im through the worst of it my lord I am glad of that. I will keep taking the tablets like I am told I try to think happy thoughts.

A week under watch, a day in a classroom talking about my life after alcohol "the rest of my life" In the treatment they explained that the reason a lot of us are here is because we drank too much but it wasn't like that for me George I did what got me here when I was much younger didn't I the drink had nothing to do with it. Well maybe something if we are being honest, They tell us we need to find something to replace the drink but I cant think of anything else its what made me like this. Next day I was sent to this cell on D wing. Theres two tables two chairs two cupboards with no locks. I don't suppose it matters for me Ive not got much. There is a toilet so its not buckets but theres only half a wall covering it up.

Im called names I suppose its understandable and fair enough. Smelly Brother come out the paper. Plastic Ripper Jack the twat I can't really complain about that can I I signed them letters. Some of the younger lads are cruder than that George you can't blame them really. Soon enough theres someone new and they shout at him instead. There was a Pakistani they call the terrorist When he arrived everyone forgot about me. Theres only one or two of the younger lads who still pull my chain George still call me plastic jack but theyre dangerous men angry men so theyre fine getting on with that.

There is a lot to take in. After Wakefield I was taken to magistrates court in a police car and charged didn't say much just my name. Entered no plea because mr Hamilos said not to. I was taken down to cells there then picked up in a van from Wakefield that went round the houses Huddersfield Bradford on the way to Leeds gaol. Stripped on the way in it was like in the films take all your clothes off and give them here. Posters for treatment courses its never too late to start the six book challenge support our antifascist prisoners. Interviews. They asked us everything about health everything about what had happened so far. All procedure. I was given things to sign compacts agreements. Sign up to your own life in prison. They give us stuff for the bed a washed bedroll. I was given new clothes at Wakefield and Ive got some more for here. Even pants and socks toothpaste. They are very thorough and the staff on the first night centre were as nice as could be.

I am due in court in January till then I am on remand. Today I was taken to video court in here. Its just a room with a table and chair and a camera on the table officers stand behind screens so they don't show up. I made my appearance in Leeds crown court on the telly. It was a short hearing so I did not need to be there in person just my presence on a telly required. I didn't say much just nodded in all the right bits George it was a bit like my wedding. The end result was the same I have been denied bail. My trial is set for next year seems a long way off but they say they need that long to prepare the case.

All best to you and yours,

Jack

PE8133 HMP Armley, Leeds, 2nd November 2005

To Sunderland Council Housing Department,

I am writing to ask after my brother Stanley who was living with me at ▮▮▮▮▮▮ Road Sunderland when I was arrested by West Yorkshire Police last month. I am his brother and I am in Leeds gaol. I have tried phoning him but the line has been cut off I have tried writing but have had no reply.

I would like to know where to go when I get out. So please help me or I will have nowhere to go except a hostel.

Yours sincerely,

John Humble

Department for Housing
Sunderland City Council
Civic Centre
Burdon Road
Sunderland
SR2 7DN

10/11/2005

Ref: AL/902/76DT

Dear Mr Humble,

An eviction notice was served on the tenants of the council property at ██████████ Road on 26th October this year. Following the arrest of one of the tenants, police reported to the council housing department the poor condition of the premises and on 24th October the property was inspected by council bailiffs and a number of serious violations of the terms of the tenancy agreement were recorded.

The sole occupant at the time of the inspection, Stanley Humble, was re-housed in temporary accommodation. Please send any post for the attention of Stanley Humble to PO Box 102, Civic Centre, Burdon Road, Sunderland, SR2 7DN, from which address it will be forwarded to his current residence.

Your sincerely,
Marjorie Robson

PE8133 HMP Armley, Leeds, 8th November 2005

Dear Stanley,

The council have written that they can send this on to you. I hope you are alright in the hostel I hope you will not be there for to long. You need to get your name down on the list for a new house.

It has been a very strange time Stanley. I didn't know what they had taken me in for at first. The time they are talking about was a long time ago. I am sure you will know all about why I have been arrested you must have read the papers. I have a lawyer and I have been told not to discuss my case with anyone.

I am here in Leeds gaol. I have been on the wing for prisoners with health problems because of the drinking. I am not allowed a drink in here, You will probably know that. They have given me some pills and I have had some sessions with counsellors but its not easy. You should look after yourself for your own sake not mine Stanley.

I suppose you will speak with Cora. Please tell her I am alright. I would be surprised if she wants to write to me right now but you can give her this address.

Keep eating plenty of food and try to go for walks and get some fresh air and exercise. Take good care of the cats and let me know if anything happens to any of them. I hope you are having no trouble off anybody and the press have gone and giving up bothering you. I am alright. I get shouted names sometimes but it is understandable. After my trial I am to try to get sent to a northern gaol if I am found guilty.

Your brother,

John

PE8133 HMP Armley, Leeds, 8th November 2005

Dear George,

I had a bad dream last night. I have been having dreams ever since coming to gaol not enough drink is the problem. The doctor said this might happen said I would not sleep well with withdrawal. I never had any dreams before not that I can remember. Always slept like a bairn Up to me neck in me own shit. Thats an old joke that is George but jokes are for sharing and its only old if youve not heard it before.

This dream was me in my cell only it wasn't my cell it was kayll road library. I was in between shelfs looking at books trying to find the right one I kept looking but I couldn't find the one I was after. In this dream I was getting more bothered more I looked and it felt like the shelfs were closing in on us I started getting panicked and tried to make a noise but nothing would come out I wanted to shout the librarian but couldn't get a sound out and still the shelfs were coming closer and closer pushing against my face Then it looked like all the books on the shelfs were the same book all of them said down the side I'm Jack that book about me only it wasn't really me was it. I started pulling them off the shelfs so I could see through to the other side and they all had pictures of me on the front but it wasn't really me it was peter Sutcliffe it was jack the ripper as the shelfs pushed in I opened up one of these books and the second the pages were open it started shouting at me in my voice shouting the words off the tape I'm Jack I'm Jack I'm Jack and all the librarians were shushing me and it wasn't me.

When I woke up Howie was holding us George I was shaking and shivering and Howie was giving us a cuddle and saying there there its just a dream. He says he only did it cause he wanted to get back to sleep but I think he is a kind man at heart.

I'm worried about Stanley george. I wrote him at home and had no reply I was worried the council might of taken the house away from him because of me. They don't need much excuse to take your council house away from you George and this might have been the excuse they needed. I asked my new lawyer mr Thomas when he came to discuss my case last week but he said that he didn't know anything about that kind of law and I needed to speak to citizens advice, I only know the one guard to speak to so I asked him and he got me a meeting with an advice counsellor. She said I had to write to the council and gave me the address and some paper and envelopes and some stamps. So I wrote to the council to say I was Stanley's brother and to ask if they knew where he was. I need to know where to go when I get out cause I am already thinking of that George all the time. I was right George theyve kicked Stanley out thats my fault and all.

I just told you about my first interview Well the second one was worse for me. Its not easy talking about something thats been bottled up that long George. It doesn't come out easy it comes out like a mess it comes out with bad blood it comes up like poison. I had to be sick in that interview room I threw my guts up in the bin in there. It wouldn't stop coming it was awful George I thought I would die. I didn't have time to get to the toilet and I wasn't sure I could ask. I was telling them everything I could then but they let me have another break after I was sick the appropriate adult Katherine was very worried George I don't think she'd ever seen anyone puke like that.

Ill tell you everything I told them in that room George Ill spill my guts again just for you. We did two interviews that night and one more the next morning and I told them everything I could Aye it was me what done it. The next morning they played us the tape and had us read it for the camera I hardly need to remind you of those words I can picture your face just reading them here.

With fond memories,

Jack the Ripper

West Yorkshire Police
Record of interview with John Samuel Humble at
Wood Street Police Station, Wakefield, 20th October 2005
Interview commencing 10.43

DS Gavin Weale: John, I'm not going to go over everything we talked about last night with regard to the letters but before we continue I would like to check that there's nothing you'd like to change from the statement you gave yesterday.

Mr Humble: No, that's the lot. I've said everything I can remember.

DS Gavin Weale: Okay, John, I realise that it's a long time ago but I'd be grateful if you would continue to try to remember as much as you can. We'd like to get as detailed account of what happened as possible.

Mr Humble: Fair enough.

DS Gavin Weale: This morning I'd like to talk to you about the tape. Is that okay with you?

Mr Humble: Aye, that's fine.

DS Gavin Weale: Thank you, John. Could you have a look at the text on this sheet please.

[DS Gavin Weale hands sheet of paper to Mr Humble]

DS Gavin Weale: Is that legible to you, John? Can you read that okay?

Mr Humble: Aye.

DS Gavin Weale: Please take your time, John, there's no hurry. I'd like you to read it all the way through. The text is the text of the words spoken on the tape sent to George Oldfield and we need you to read it for verification purposes. As I say, please take your time reading it through and start whenever you're ready.

Mr Humble: I'm Jack. I see you are still having no luck catching me. I have the greatest respect for you, George, but Lord, you are no nearer to catching me now than four years ago when I started. I reckon your boys are letting you down, George.

You can't be much good, can you? The only time they came near catching me was a few months back in Chapeltown when I was disturbed. Even then it was a uniform copper, not a detective.

I warned you in March that I'd strike again, sorry it wasn't Bradford, I did promise you that but I couldn't get there. I'm not sure when I will strike again but it will definitely be some time this year, maybe September or October, even soon if I get the chance. I'm not sure where. Maybe Manchester; I like there, there's plenty of them knocking about. They never learn, do they, George? I bet you've warned them, but they never listen. At the rate I'm going I should be in the book of records, I think it's eleven up to now, isn't it? Well, I'll keep on going for quite a while yet. I can't see myself being nicked just yet. Even if you do get near, I'll probably top myself first.

Well, it's been nice chatting to you, George. Yours, Jack the Ripper.

No good looking for fingerprints, you should know by now it's clean as a whistle. See you soon. 'Bye. Hope you like the catchy tune at the end. Ha-ha!

DS Gavin Weale: Gill, could you play the original recording for comparison?

[DC Gill Partington activates tape recording]

[I'm Jack. I see you are still having no luck catching me. I have the greatest respect for you, George, but Lord, you are no nearer to catching me now than four years ago when I started. I reckon your boys are letting you down, George.

You can't be much good, can you? The only time they came near catching me was a few months back in Chapeltown when I was disturbed. Even then it was a uniform copper, not a detective.

I warned you in March that I'd strike again, sorry it wasn't Bradford, I did promise you that but I couldn't get there. I'm not sure when I will strike again but it will definitely be some time this year, maybe September or October, even soon if I get the chance. I'm not sure where. Maybe Manchester; I like there, there's plenty of them knocking about. They never learn, do they, George? I bet you've warned them, but they never listen. At the rate I'm going I should be in the book of records, I think it's eleven up to now, isn't it? Well, I'll keep on going for quite a while yet. I can't see myself being nicked just yet. Even if you do get near, I'll probably top myself first.

Well, it's been nice chatting to you, George. Yours, Jack the Ripper.

No good looking for fingerprints, you should know by now it's clean as a whistle. See you soon. 'Bye. Hope you like the catchy tune at the end. Ha-ha!]

DS Gavin Weale: John, I'm going to ask you directly, were you responsible for producing that tape?

Mr Humble: Aye, it was me. It was my voice. Was eerie, like, wasn't it? Must have been mad. I feel crap.

DS Gavin Weale: Why do you feel crap?

Mr Humble: For putting the coppers off in a way. I did have respect for George, like, you know, George Oldfield. I said that on the tape, didn't I? I did have respect for him anyway. And he was turning older by the day. Did you not see his face when he was on the telly? He looked old because he had all the worry on him.

DS Gavin Weale: What effect do you think this tape had?

Mr Humble: I don't know. Don't know. I shouldn't have done it, like. I know that. Because it's evil, it sounds evil. I just didn't realise about my accent, that's what misled the police. My accent. Anybody could have sent the letters. I know there was no way of checking that. But once they got my accent, I realised that. That's why I phoned in to try to tell them "Don't look for a Geordie" but they didn't take any notice.

PE8133 HMP Armley, Leeds, 23rd November 2005

Dear George,

Another bad dream last night but no rats. I was shouting in my sleep when I woke up. Howie didn't give us a hug this time he told us to grow the fuck up.

I do not leave my cell much George just to get food have a shower exercise twice a week. I cannot apply for work because I am on remand. I cannot do much when I am on remand. A lot of the lads in this gaol are only on remand theres just one or two like Howie on longer sentences. He says its not meant for people like him, I'm not sure its meant for anyone this gaol George its seen better days thats certain.

Ive been reading as much as I used to when I was a lad. Wer'e banged up so long even telly gets boring you just need a change, There was a lad came round with a trolley of books told us about the library said how good it was. Ive borrowed a stack of books off this lad. I said I used to read mainly crime stuff or horror and he just laughed. You and everybugger else. He said to try Arthur Conan Doyle who wrote the Sherlock Holmes books. Youve got to laugh I think he was taking the piss. Ive never actually read any of that only seen the tv and films. Ive got the first ever holmes book and some other old detective stories. Ive got some new crime ones. The lad said here try this Alan Silitoe yorkshire writer its about borstal. Got some horror stuff Stephen king and dracula.

Judge Norman Jones wouldn't give me bail I don't know why George Ive nowhere to run to Ive never left Sunderland till Ive been brought to Leeds gaol apart from medomsley holiday one year at seahouses. I get lots of visitors here but they are all lawyers Not the kind Id like.

We have been going through my life history me and my lawyer. He says the jury wont know what we dont tell them but that the prosecution will try to make me sound like a villain and it will help if we can tell a different story. He says that if he can get them on our side they will more likely let me off. Im not one for sob stories George I told my own version.

Me and Stanley used to love playing on the street when we was bairns knicky knocky nine doors trespassing in peoples gardens. We used to play this game where one of you was standing on one side of the road and one of you on the other and you pretended you were having a tug of war both pretended you were pulling a rope but there was nothing there. You had to really put your back into it George to make it look real you had to pull that invisible rope for all your life. It was best on chester road we pulled our rope when there was a car coming there wasn't so many of them back then George you could be waiting minutes or more but then youd get one a ford anglia a sports car if you were lucky cause theyd be going faster some of them would just drive through theyd seen it all before or they didn't care but some of them as soon as they saw you theyd slam on the brakes come skidding down the road. it was a hoot that man George wed' wet ourselves at that sometimes they left skidmarks then we'd have to scarper and jump over the wall into the crem hide behind gravestones. This one time we did it to a bus honest George I thought it was going to topple over there was biddies screaming on the top deck. the driver come running out the front shouting come here you hooligans Im calling the police don't think youre getting away with this we were over that wall and away right down the far end of the crem he did call the police Jammer saw your lot all along the road later that after but we stayed home they were never going to catch us George.

Not then maybe but later. Ive had a few scrapes with the law. Burglary once. Going equipped another time. I was only fifteen trying to break in to a pub Of course it was where else. Just me and Geoff Hewson, Getting nicked for carrying a hammer and a crowbar seems a bit stiff doesn't it. Youd probably not think so being a copper. Got off with a probation warning that time and a braying off our mam.

Burglary was a bakery on Pennywell Road. It was a great job that me and Mike Moody. Foggy night we were just kicking our heels wandering around brassic and bored looking for something to do. Our mam had kicked us out the house to do something else than watch telly. I don't know who spotted the open window first. Mike was chunky like and I was skinny so Mike give us a bunk over the wall and I was in like Flynn. I opened the gate for Mike and we went through that bakers office like nobodys business. Found a cashbox but not a lot else. Getting it back home was the difficult bit in past my mam but she was sat watching telly with a whisky and ginger so it wasn't so hard. Took it up to my room and got into it with a hammer and chisel. Seventy eight pounds fifteen and fourpence hapenny. I remember that cause they made a big fuss of it in magistrates court had the accounts and everything.

It was a good haul but we weren't daft. Mike wanted to blow it all but I said wed attract suspicion if we did that. So I stashed in a drainpipe after that. Sure enough coppers come round knocking Already had a reputation didn't I. But I was nice as pie nothing to do with me officer. My mam was nice and polite My boy was here all night officer then give us hell as soon as copper was gone. What have you been up to you little bastard. It all would of been fine if he hadnt come back when it was raining all that lovely spond come sloshing out of the drainpipe right in front of his eyes George.

Had to try and keep me nose clean after that one but its easier said than done. When I was nineteen I got sent down to borstal at medomsley which is near to consett out in county durham. Used to be in that advert for phileas fogg crisps made in consett county durham. Thered been a fight George, Id won but that doesn't stop you getting nicked does it. I don't remember much but mr Thomass got the old statements. This fight though George at the mecca The lad I had a go with was one of your lot. He didn't tell me that before did he. Not really fair warning. It was a stitch up George All the police statements agreed it was me what started it.

Your friend

Jack Jack Jack

Form MGHA(T)

Witness Statement

(CJ Act 1967, s.9 MC Act 1960, ss. (5A)3a and 5B. MC Rules 1961, r.70)

Statement of: **John Samuel Humble**

Age if under 18: 'over 18' (if over 18 insert 'over 18')

Occupation: Unemployed

This statement (consisting of 2 pages each signed by me) is true to the best of my knowledge and belief and I make it knowing that, if it is tendered in evidence, I shall be liable to prosecution if I have wilfully stated in it anything which I know to be false or do not believe to be true.

Signature:

It was a Friday night and I'd wanted to go out but there was no one around. My brother Stanley was away at Catterick and none of the girls wanted to come with me. I didn't have much money so I'd bought a bottle of vodka from the shops and drunk it in my room listening to a record. I think it was Mud. I'd gone down into town and had a quick drink at The Barley Mow pub hoping to meet someone there but there was no one I knew. I suppose I had a pint or two there. I'd gone over the water and on to the Mecca on my own, walked all the way stopped off for a pint on the way. I can't remember where. As I was walking up the ramp past the bouncers I realised how pissed I was but they let me in anyway. I fell over on the dancefloor but I got back up holding on to the trunk of one of the trees they've got. I guess that's why they've got trees in the middle of the dancefloor. I'd started dancing because they were playing that song that goes: "That's right that's right that's right that's right." I love that song. I was listening to it just before I went out.

I'd bumped into another lad on the dancefloor and he got dead aggressive straightaway. He says to watch out and I've said to mind his own business. He's said "What?" So I said "You heard." He spun round and said: "Say that again." I said "Just leave it." He said: "You should leave." I said: "Who says?" He replied: "Seriously, you should leave before you do yourself an injury. It's just gone nine o'clock and you're blotto." I was scared that this lad was going to start on us so I left the dancefloor and went to the bar.

There was this girl at the bar. She was dead bonny so I asked her for a dance. They were playing "Do the Jukebox Jive". She said "You couldn't dance if you wanted." I said "I've got all the moves pet" and I did a spin. It was class but she pretended she wasn't impressed.

I saw the girl from before on the dancefloor and danced towards her. The guy in the song was singing "Zoo time is she and you time". I asked her if she liked my dancing. Heartbeat, increasing heartbeat. She spat at us. Can you believe that? She spat at us for no reason. The man was singing "You hear the thunder of stampeding rhinos, elephants and tacky tigers".

I wanted to slap her, teach her a lesson, but I didn't, I held back. One of the lads with her punched us and I fell to the floor. I grabbed for this lad's legs and he fell over. A crowd gathered round us on the dancefloor and they were egging us on to hit him.

I wouldn't normally have done anything but I was on my own and I felt like they were ganging up on us. The song was going "As twenty cannibals have hold of you, they need their protein just like you do".

That's when I saw the bouncers coming. I tried to get up on my own but they picked us up before I could stand. I think I shouted at them I can't really remember. I was probably in shock. They carried me to a room off the main dancefloor where they held us against my will until the police arrived. The bouncers threatened us with physical violence and called us all sorts of names, a twat and a prick. I don't want to press charges against them because I'm scared that they would come looking for us.

Form MGHA(T)

Witness Statement

(CJ Act 1967, s.9 MC Act 1960, ss. (5A)3a and 5B. MC Rules 1961, r.70)

Statement of: **PC David Smythe**

Age if under 18: 'over 18' (if over 18 insert 'over 18')

Occupation: Police Constable

This statement (consisting of 1 page signed by me) is true to the best of my knowledge and belief and I make it knowing that, if it is tendered in evidence, I shall be liable to prosecution if I have wilfully stated in it anything which I know to be false or do not believe to be true.

Signature:

I arrived at the Locarno Ballrooms, colloquially known as the Mecca, with a group of five friends at approximately 9.10 p.m. on the evening of the 25th. We had previously been at the bar upstairs, Genevieve's, where we had been enjoying a quiet evening. I had drunk two bottles of Newcastle Brown Ale.

Immediately on entering the Locarno Ballrooms, which was not yet very busy, we all noticed one man who was extremely inebriated and repeatedly stumbling and falling over on the dancefloor. One of the friends with whom I'd arrived, Olwen

Robertson, suggested that I speak to the gentleman and ask him to leave. I explained that I would rather enjoy my night off but when he subsequently stumbled into me I advised the man that given his state he should go home. He swore at me and left the dancefloor for the bar. I carried on dancing with my friends.

At approximately 9.30 p.m. the drunken man came back on to the dancefloor and grabbed hold of Olwen, despite her protestations. He then slapped her. I immediately took hold of his arm and attempted an armlock at which point he punched me. I threw him to the ground, whereupon he grabbed hold of my legs and pulled me down. He jumped to his feet and started kicking my face and head. I did not see what happened at this stage because I was attempting to protect my face and head with my arms. Once the bouncers had removed the man my friends helped me to a table and inspected my injuries – a number of cuts to the face inflicted by the man's boots. On the arrival of the ambulance I was urged to attend A&E at Sunderland General to have the cuts seen to. I gave a brief statement to the officers at the scene before going to the hospital in the ambulance.

Form MGHA(T)

Witness Statement

(CJ Act 1967, s.9 MC Act 1960, ss. (5A)3a and 5B. MC Rules 1961, r.70)

Statement of: **Olwen Robertson**

Age if under 18: 'over 18' (if over 18 insert 'over 18')

Occupation: Dental nurse

This statement (consisting of 1 page signed by me) is true to the best of my knowledge and belief and I make it knowing that, if it is tendered in evidence, I shall be liable to prosecution if I have wilfully stated in it anything which I know to be false or do not believe to be true.

Signature:

I've never experienced anything quite like it. It was absolutely awful. We'd been upstairs in Genevieve's having a really nice night, a group of pals, and then we came downstairs to the Mecca. There was this one lad who was absolutely paralytic drunk already in there. I asked Dave (PC Smythe) to have a word because I was quite worried about him. He looked like he might hurt himself. Dave wasn't going to say anything, I don't think he wanted the bother when he was off-duty, but this lad smashed into him on the dancefloor – nothing agro, just clumsy, like. So

Dave did have a word then, along the lines of, really, marrah, look after yourself. This lad leaves the dancefloor but he was back a couple of songs later and he danced straight up to me and grabbed hold of my arm. He leant right in and said "I bet you'd fucking love it off me, pet. How about it?" I told him where to stick that and he slapped me. I couldn't believe it, it really hurt, but then before I knew it he was trying to punch Dave. Dave got him to the ground but this lad tripped Dave up and jumped up and started kicking him. We were all screaming at him to stop, it was absolutely terrifying, he was like a wild animal. It was horrible. The bouncers arrived pretty quickly and dragged him off. Poor Dave was in a right state. I think his pride was hurt more than anything else. Honestly, I've never seen anything like it, this lad was a psycho.

Form MGHA(T)

Witness Statement

(CJ Act 1967, s.9 MC Act 1960, ss. (5A)3a and 5B. MC Rules 1961, r.70)

Statement of: **Micky Finn**

Age if under 18: 'over 18' (if over 18 insert 'over 18')

Occupation: Security

This statement (consisting of 1 page signed by me) is true to the best of my knowledge and belief and I make it knowing that, if it is tendered in evidence, I shall be liable to prosecution if I have wilfully stated in it anything which I know to be false or do not believe to be true.

Signature:

Friday nights are always the worst. People get demob happy, don't they? Me and Arthur heard the screaming and sprinted straight over to where the trouble was. I pushed my way through the crowd and saw the suspect – he is a suspect, isn't he? – stood over another lad and putting the boot in. That's not on, that. We didn't muck about; we picked him up and took him straight out back kicking and screaming. I've done self-defence in the army so I knew how to keep him in a pressure hold. I asked Gary [the barman] to call the police and ambulance. In the back room the suspect was screaming blue murder, effing this effing that, twat this prick that. Me and Arthur just laughed it off, to be honest. I mean he's a skinny little toerag, isn't he? Not much of a threat to a couple of lumps like us. I told him he was barred for life and that we'd called the police. I hope he gets what he deserves, to be honest.

Form MGHA(T)

Witness Statement

(CJ Act 1967, s.9 MC Act 1960, ss. (5A)3a and 5B. MC Rules 1961, r.70)

Statement of: **Arthur Runcorn**

Age if under 18: 'over 18' (if over 18 insert 'over 18')

Occupation: Nightclub bouncer

This statement (consisting of 1 page signed by me) is true to the best of my knowledge and belief and I make it knowing that, if it is tendered in evidence, I shall be liable to prosecution if I have wilfully stated in it anything which I know to be false or do not believe to be true.

Signature:

I'm not sure I'll be able to tell you much more than what Mick's said. The lad was out of order. He was mortal as well. I've not seen him before. I didn't let him in. It was Mick on the main door. I was doing the stairs down from Gen's. He got a proper doing the other lad though. Is he alright? The other lad?

Dear George,

At the trial back then my lawyer told the magistrates it was the other lad had thrown the first punch but they weren't interested. He said I'd been put upon by an offduty policeman and they'd fixed all the evidence against me but the magistrates said I was lucky not be sent to Crown Court cause Id used my feet. because it was my first violent offence they were going to deal with it themselves. What my lawyer said about the statements had been true George. The police had fixed them all up so their lad didn't look bad. everyone agreed I was the wrong'un. They sentenced me to three month custodial sentence and told me I was lucky they could have handed down 12. I didn't feel lucky George I can tell you that. My mam cried in court George and Cora looked at us like I were nowt. Stanley wasn't there was he he was in Catterick.

I suppose you have a pretty good idea of what it was like in borstal you being a copper. I had heard all sorts about borstal but it was worse than anyone had said. They had us in swaddie uniforms and doing square bashing marching drill and that. They had us swimming in cold pools and cold showers and cold baths with no trunks on The bosses didn't like trunks George. They had us boxing and playing rugby and doing running all of it was for our own good to make us into real men "honest men". The lads beat each other up. There was screws favourites could do what they want and dormitory bosses. They were worse bastards sometimes than the bosses themselves. The punishment just came down from one to the next.

I suppose I was a lucky one because I was fast at running. Not just a bit fast George really fast. I felt free when I was running over the moors at consett trot-trot-trot slap-slap-slap all sorts going through my head. I used to go out in the morning first thing when no one else was up all cold in my vest and shorts I felt like I was the only person on the earth running around then or sometimes the last person on the earth like everyone else was dead I don't know which was worst. You don't look like you ever did much running even for a bus George that rosy face of yours. Youd of been out of puff but I loved that the air going deep in my lungs in out in out one eye on the track ahead one eye on the ground in front of my feet not wanting to get tripped up by brambles and branches just keep on going first mile or two always a bit sticky but after that George I always found peace. No thoughts you didn't want A real clear head like the cold air was coming in and your foggy breath was blowing it out cleaning it all up all that stuff that made us angry stuff about coppers George about your lot about people letting us down about people I wanted to wallop None of that when I was running George just one foot in front of the other freedom even if I was in prison. It was a long game just stick with it even if you feel slow or tired just stick with it and the run finds you the pace finds you. I used to like going uphill better than going down George I know that sounds daft but its true you had to keep everything under control coming downhill couldn't let your legs just run or theyd run away without you youd' come a right cropper arms all over the place Trying to keep balance. Uphill you just pump pump pump breathe

breathe breathe eyes down keep going and every time when you come back down youd think I never went that far up did I?

I was faster than the rest of the lads George so The governor wanted me to race in this big race against another borstal in Northumberland. I didn't want to do anything to make him happy that old bastard so I had a plan George I kept it to myself wouldn't of worked if Id told another soul. I was winning the race against this lad from Northumberland eight miles long and everyone was cheering us in and then just before we got the finish line I slowed right down and let him past I just stopped going so fast. Id won it already George Id showed I d won I know Id won everyone knew Id won but then I just seemed to go backwards. it was quite hard to be honest its not easy to lose when you'r'e that fast you have to put in the effort but it was worth it. That showed the governor George. He was raging at that but he couldnt get me to do what he wanted I won at their game George. Showed them who was dear boss.

Thing is George really I am as honest as him. I have my honesty and he has his honesty. He wanted us all to come out honest men but at the same time he ran a rotten shop George rotten to the core. Whos to say whats honest. I don't think theres anyone fit to judge not even the judge in that court room I bet hes got some skeletons too who doesn't.

This should be the bit where I give you the sob story about how my dad died and how I found him in his room but I cant do that Im not playing your game either George.

Most of the lads in there had no family god I'm glad I had family. It was a lot worse if you didn't have a mam to come visit at weekends no one to tell what they did to you. There was lads died while I was at medomsley George. Not just

the ones that topped themselves. everyone knew why George
but no one was getting punished, People talk about justice
Ive not seen a lot.

Yours sincerely

Jack

PE8133 HMP Armley, Leeds, 10th January 2006

Dear George,

Yesterday was a busy day George I was in Crown Court to lodge a plea of not guilty. I was picked up from gaol by a van and taken for my hearing with another lad who was in court in the morning. I was given some clothes for court so I would not have to be in my jeans and sweatshirt. It was better than looking shabby but it smelt of wet washing.

I went straight into a meeting with Mr Thomas and I tried to help him as much as possible. The Crown prosecution Service will charge me with four counts of perverting the course of justice. I have said all along to Mr Thomas that I cant remember writing all the letters because I was that drunk so I will plead not guilty. Mr Thomas was not convinced that it was a good idea but he said he would argue as he was instructed and that it was my right to make this defence.

In the hearing the prosecution said what evidence they had to present. He was called Richard Foster. They have handwriting voice fingerprint blood and DNA. The prosecution has all those bits of me George. I am not sure where the fingerprints are from because they lost the tape for so long and I wiped it clean. I told this to mr Thomas afterwards and he said that was good useful information for our witnesses to look into. The blood is from saliva blood type. Ive never knew my own blood type till I heard it on the news back then. Wasn't going to tell DS Weale was I. Quite rare B secretor George. But you knew all about that that was your big lead wasn't it.

Mr Thomas said we would do our own handwriting and voice analysis to go against theirs. The DNA he says it can be argued that it is not certain because it is still a new science He can find an expert witness. Mr Thomas has advised me that it will be difficult to prove that I was so drunk I could not remember writing the letter and putting it in an envelope and then posting it three times over and then recording a tape and then putting that in a letter and then posting that. He doesn't think well be able to persuade a jury especially given my confession. Mr Thomas thinks it will be better to say that it cannot be proved that I intended to mislead you George. I do not wish to plead guilty George I am innocent of perverting the course of justice.

Mr Thomas is quite a scary man George I think he will be good for my side but I can see he is not certain about our case. I will hope for the best.

Yours hopefully

Jack

PE8133 HMP Armley, Leeds, 1st February 2006

Dear George,

I had two visitors today Mr Windsor Lewis An expert for the defence and his assistant some lad. He has been involved in this case for a long time I remembered his name George. He was one of your experts the first time round. He went on the news after they took you off the case and put Dick Hobson on. He didn't agree that my accent was put on and that I had a speech impediment. He said there was lots of speech experts that didn't agree. He was right and all so I am glad he is on my side this time.

I didn't tell him I knew who he was. I did as I was asked George. He seemed like a decent man "just doing his job".

The room was crap. There was a small table and two chairs and only one lamp and it was knackered The small window did not give much light at all. There weren't any sockets for them to plug their gear into. I could tell Mr Lewis was a bit cross about this but he was still polite. I asked how come he was on my side and he said I've been asked to prepare a report by your legal team to assess the weight of the claim that you made the tape and wrote the letters. I asked what this meant and he said I need to check if your voice matches up with the recording and your writing with the letters. I said well it does doesn't it. And he said That may well be true Mr Humble but the prosecution might be saying that it does for the wrong reasons.

We chatted quite a lot George between me reading out the tape for all his fancy recording gear. I told him about where I come from and about my family. He didn't really believe that no one I lived with could ever have recognised me but I told him it was true Not Stanley not Cora not anyone. He thought it was odd that Id never learnt to drive but I told him Id never needed to. Everything I needed was in Sunderland. I told him about my life and he was interested in jobs. I said I hadn't had that many but I did tell him about Howson taking the piss when I went on as an apprentice brickie. He dint understand that at first because of my accent I beg your pardon he said. I said Dont you understand Geordie then. He liked that one George a man with a sense of humour.

He had me copy out the letters as well Like school dictation. It wasn't bad Got me out of my cell. I said I hoped I would see him again soon like I hope I will write to you again soon as I have some more news.

Yours

Jack

In the original versions of the hoax letters there were a variety of idiosyncratic spellings, capitalisations and intra-word spacings. In the Armley dictated versions there were similar but irregular occurrences of such features. It was very likely that the original-letter spelling "nite" was likely to have been relatively jokey because the orthodox "night" was used at Armley. The original two occurrences of "respectfully" now both become "respectively". This suggested poor linguistic judgement as did his apparent lack of realisation that his accent could be identified by large numbers of people within a very narrowly definable area of England.

Among the various points that I noted were the fact that the word "cursed" which in the original letter had been spelt "curserred" was now written with a single instead of a double "r". Its unstressed vowel's spelling no doubt reflected the "obscure" value the region has in such syllables. The form "cursen" of the original letter now had a less archaic appearance as "cursing". Apostrophes and spacings were often employed differently from the ways they appeared in the originals but not with any regular system.

A particularly notable difference between the original letters and the defendant's writing out of them at Armley lay in the fact that on at least three occurrences of the five uses of the numeral "7" in the original letters there was to be seen the mid-height horizontal cross-bar that characterises the widespread Continental but rarely if ever found British usage. None of the Armley five occurrences showed this treatment. Of course such a pattern may simply indicate the subsequent dropping of an earlier habit and it may even have been noticed by Humble that attention had been drawn to this usage in the press so that he now deliberately resisted such a tendency. The pronunciations occurring in his readings of the text of the original hoax message likewise revealed no very significant discrepancies between that original and the newly made recordings.

Conclusion

My overall impression from intensive examination of the Armley versions of the letters and recordings is that there is no cogent evidence that could be adduced to claim that the accused has not been responsible for the actions with which he is charged.

PE8133 HMP Armley, Leeds, 8th February 2006

Dear George,

The biggest problem in here is getting bored. We watch a
lot of telly Howie and me we are on bangup nearly 20 hours
a day right now only out for exercise and meals. The food is
alright but is often cold and not enough. We get given our
breakfast at evening canteen and everyone eats it straightaway.

The days pass slowly except for TV. We watch all the chat
programmes and news programmes and any good films. It is
even worse at weekends we hardly get out of the cells at all.
Association is one hour and if youre my age theres no football
or anything and theres always arguments over the pool table
Theres a crowd of Asian lads from the twos always manage to
get their first and fix up the rota and then theres all kinds of
argie bargie Paki this paki that. I keep away from that.

Mr Thomas has told me of the crowns plans to bring expert
witnesses which was why he had mr Windsor Lewis visit me.
People have listened to my voice and examined my tape. Dr
Peter French and Dr Philip Harrison did the forensic analysis
of my tape Mr Thomas showed me an example of their work.
My Lord it is complicated but they know all about what they're
doing and what Im saying. Did you even know what a consonant is George. You were more of a thieftaker weren't you not
much of a one for analysis.

Mr Thomas says that Mr Windsor lewis cant help us so we will argue against the evidence by saying that it should not be presented. I am not sure I understand why but I think it is because it doesn't say anything new if I am already confessing to it. He says their evidence is about identity They will try to prove it was my voice and I have already admitted that. He will ask that my DNA is not brought into court evidence for the same reason. I said Id be bringing it whether he liked it or not He didn't think that was funny. He says we should make it only a question of intent and he has asked for a fresh hearing so that we can alter the plea.

He says that is why he will try to make them understand why I did it How Id had a hard life. He says the jury will not know about my previous which is just as well even tho it was all that long ago. He has asked me to tell him more about why I did it. About giving you a kick up the arse.

There are lots of reasons George. I was bored and on the dole and drunk. The inquiry was getting on my nerves. It was always on the telly so I thought I'd boost it up a bit. I wanted someone to listen to me because no one ever does. I sent the letter to the Mirror for the publicity but I didn't want to get caught. I did have respect for you george but I could see you getting older by the day. You had all that worry on your back. I didn't realise at the time what a serious thing it was. I think I deserve to go to jail for it for writing those letters. I think I deserve to go to jail for at least two years.

Yours respectfully

Jack

Exhibit reference CS 183254 (Crown submission)
Report of Doctor Peter French, J. P. French and Associates

Segmental features

We found no significant differences between the vowel and consonant realisations in the two samples and we concluded that the accent was the same. However, over and above the social and regional features that were common to the recordings there was a cluster of features of a more personally distinguishing nature. This sporadic use of [d] for /ð/ word-initially (not a feature expected from the area – see Figures 1 and 2) devoicing of word-final lenis consonants (e.g. 'George' final /dʒ/→[tʃ]) and a tendency, in utterance-final position, for fortis plosives to be given a somewhat sustained hold phase prior to prominent release (e.g. 'I'm Jack' final /k/→[kːʰ] – see Figure 5).

Multiple instances of the same vowel phonemes were identified. Their formats were tracked and the values logged and plotted. A high degree of overlap was found for groupings of f3 values across the recordings, as well as for f1 and f2, as shown in respect of /iː/, /ɪ/, /e/ and /a/ in Figures 3 and 4.

Suprasegmental features

In terms of rhythm and intonation, we again found no difference that we considered diagnostic of a different speaker, although it must be said that one might expect few such differences to arise even if different speakers had been involved, as the content of the read passages was the same and the line layout of the transcript read by

Humble had previously been based on the pausing behaviour found in the hoax recording.

With regard to voice quality, the following features were noted as common to both samples: high degree of nasality, supra-laryngeal tension, breathiness, creakiness – albeit the degree of the latter feature was somewhat lower in the known recording than in the hoax.

Average fundamental frequency was calculated at 100Hz for the hoax recording and 115 Hz for the reference material. Interestingly, given that the defendant was 49 years old at the time of providing the reference sample, the prediction from the research literature would have been that at the time of the hoax recordings his fundamental frequency would have been higher than 115Hz, had he conformed to general population trends.

Conclusion

Despite the non-contemporaneous nature of the hoax and interview recordings, very striking and distinctive points of similarity emerged from the comparison on all the dimensions examined. Phonetically and acoustically, the voice and speech patterns of the hoaxer are consistent with those of the defendant in all significant respects. Whilst, in the present state of knowledge one can never exclude the possibility of there being others in the population who would share the constellation of features common to the known and questioned recordings, in respect of these particular recordings I would consider that possibility to be a remote one.

PE8133 HMP Armley, Leeds, 24th February 2006

Dear George,

Mr Thomas has made the new submission to a different judge. He tells me he has made sure it is known we are still pleading not guilty. He says this is important because it means we can appeal and he says it will be difficult for the prosecution to prove intent because I did not mean to do any harm I was just being daft. I suppose this makes sense.

Howie thinks I should get myself a new penpal because you never write back. Ive told him Im not really interested in hearing from anyone else. He thinks Im lonely but it doesn't matter youre not really ever lonely in here George theres people everywhere all the time even when youre having a shit.

From gaol

Jack

PE8133 HMP Armley, Leeds, 17th March 2006

Dear George,

I do not want an argument anymore Im tired. I do not want a three week trial. I have decided to plead guilty to all the charges and tell the judge and jury that I am truly sorry George. I am very sorry for what I did it was a long time ago. I will tell them everything about how I made the tape. Mr Thomas says weve got a good chance of persuading them I never meant to rubbish your investigation. He says I might get let out with nothing more to serve. I don't really care George I deserve to go to prison for what I did and I don't want the fight over it for anyones sake.

Trial starts tomorrow.

Jack

PE8133 HMP Armley, Leeds, 21st March 2006

Dear George,

It is now all over and the sentencing is done. I am to serve eight years in gaol. It seems a bit much George but its not up to me. Mr bromley-hughes the lead barrister says we will appeal to get the sentence cut down. I have served nearly six months on remand so with a fixed sentence I can expect to be out on licence in four years. I suppose I deserve it It was an evil thing to do.

After I was brought back from court in the van I was taken to the reception wing and told I would be in a new cell now I am convicted On a new wing. Someone else already has my old cell there is no room anywhere since C wing is closed. They said I will have to have a new cellmate its goodbye to Howie without any goodbyes. I will miss him he was a gentle giant and its a lottery everyone crowded into cells. My new cellmate is a lad called Deafie from Peterlee he seems alright at first.

I did do it george and I admitted that in the interview There wasn't' any point in trying to deny that they had the video as evidence. It was weird to see myself on the screen sat in that room wearing the sweatshirt and trousers theyd given me and telling the tales but it was better than telling it all again. I don't think I could of done that in front of everyone George and then all the evidence the handwriting the tape recordings the speech. Was it me was it my voice How different were my voices.

There was a lot of fuss when I said I would change my plea. Mr Bromley-hughes said that it undid all their preparation. That they were sure they could prove I did not intend to mislead the investigation. I said I didn't care George and he said so be it. Mr Thomas looked very dark. We went into court and we told the judge and he dismissed the jury "twelve good men and true".

It was mostly about making arguments for mitigation after I changed my plea. It didn't seem much like mitigation to me To be honest it was more like insults. How I was a hopeless alcoholic spectacularly inadequate. I suppose the idea was to make the judge feel sorry for me. well he didn't feel that sorry did he and I didn't really get my say.

The first day was the prosecution about why I was such a evil man. Mr Horsley QC said I had an encyclopaedic knowledge of the Ripper. He said that twice george and its true. I read the Mirror and The Sun everyday Ive always clipped the newspapers Still do. He said I must of spent time on it and gone out of my way I must of read everything because there was a lot of facts from The Mirror but also the point of that one woman being in hospital had only been in the mail. I did read the mail from time to time but its not really my paper George.

They played the recordings of me and the video of my confession Mr Horsley gave all the details How I had taken out a book from Kayll road library never returned it and used words from the dear boss letters. He had a copy of the library ticket would you believe Jack the ripper a casebook. It was from a TV programme on the BBC. That was a good book that George I read it over and again.

Mr Horsley said how I wasn't arguing Id tried to deceive and how that had cost three women their lives. That was harsh George but I have worried about that myself.

Second day was mr bromley-hughes on my behalf "with friends like these". It was mr bromley-hughes told all the alkie stuff. Truth is we were living badly Stanley and me. Every day to fairleys to buy cider a lot cheaper than the pub 2.99 for 2 litres Then back home and get pissed. Not much of a life you might say but one on the outside of prison One with cider.

And the recorder judge Norman jones he had plenty to say. He thought the tape was cleverly constructed and my delivery was sinister. It takes all sorts eh george.

I was drunk and young and angry. I don't suppose you know what its like being on the dole especially when you've got a record like I had george. I was angry especially seeing other lads doing alright and theres always someone. When the papers started calling this lad doing the killing a ripper I thought I know about that better than them. I mean did you really know about the ripper george. I don't think so otherwise youd of read the dear boss letter. Im not one for cursen George but it was a fucking travesty all the reporting back then. And you lot were next to useless.

Sorry but its true

Jack

Leeds Crown Court
Official Transcription of Judge's remarks
Recorder Judge Norman Jones in the case of
R. vs John Samuel Humble

"You arrogantly set out to send the investigation away from the path of the true killer. You did that with an indifference to the potentially fatal consequences, which was breathtaking and this sets you in the most serious category of offending of this type.

"The Ripper attacked without mercy and police were baffled for five years and he remained undetected. I'm satisfied one of the factors that may well have contributed to his remaining at large for so long was you sending the letters and the tape.

"While it cannot be said that your actions caused or directly led to the murders of three women and the attacks on two other women who survived, they moved the focus of the police investigation to Sunderland. While it can neither be said with any certainty that the murderer might have been caught any earlier, we can be sure, from statements made by Peter Sutcliffe on his arrest, that the hoax letters and tape had given him confidence to continue in his course of actions.

"The least that could be said was these victims would have stood a better chance of not being attacked had these police resources been directed in West Yorkshire.

"You took on his persona. Your letters comprised a mixture of taunts and threats and were well researched. Then you sent a tape recording of you pretending to be the Ripper. It was cleverly constructed and your delivery was sinister.

"Police were persuaded that the hoaxer was the killer and you must have appreciated the way the police were being led astray. At no time did you have the courage to come forward and confess.

"You are a man with a dislike of the police and it gave you pleasure to make fools of them. What is unforgivable is that you failed to put the record straight when you realised the damage you were doing. Had that tape not been sent, the deployment to Sunderland, whether wise or not, would simply not have occurred.

"Perverting the course of justice is a serious offence because the intention of the offender is to manipulate our justice system and produce injustice.

"In this case the manner of your offending, if not unique, is almost so. You planned to manipulate the process of the investigation of one of the most horrific series of murders ever seen in this country. You warped and bent its path away from the true killer.

"For these reasons I have elected to impose the most severe sentence available to me given the charges brought. I sentence John Samuel Humble to eight years in prison for each of four counts of perverting the course of justice, the sentences to run concurrently."

PE8133 HMP Armley, Leeds, 1st April 2006

Dear George,

I have been thinking of an April fool for you George.

No prizes for guessing which newspaper is the most popular in here. We have to share one copy between about ten of us. We take turns for who gets it first and then we ask the guards to pass it on down the chain. If youre near the top of the queue you get to read the paper if youre not you don't. There is an exception to the rule if youre in the paper which means Ive been getting to read it every day this week.

I get to hear about whats in the news whether I like it or not. Vikki has sold her soul to the sun George. I cant say I blame her She doesn't owe me anything. She said she was ashamed of me when she came to visit. Im sure she didn't say all the things theyre printing about me. You know what the papers are like. I hope she got a pretty packet out of it.

I don't suppose you will know who Vikki is. Shes my ex-wife George. We were together for twelve year and some of it was good. She had two bairns from before. I treated them like my own. It all went wrong after I left my job Couldnt handle the nights George. I thought Id get something else but I never did. I suppose it must of been hard on her living on benefits. We argued a lot mostly about money and the drink. I was drinking a lot George when youre not working theres a not lot else to do. But some of the stuff shes said about me in

██████ is not right. Im getting called names all over again in here Its like when I first got in. I could understand it more then.

One thing does upset me George and that is Vikki telling them about when she came to visit. I wish she had told me then that she was speaking to the newspapers I wouldn't have said so much. She come in with Jan and they sat there looking sad It was nice to get visitors and I was touched that they had made the effort to come and see me the whole thing was not for nothing twelve years. It was not plain sailing the visit There were lots of tears and accusations but now I think it was all because the newspaper put her up to it. I cant be sure George but why else would she tell them what we said. The timing is suspicious Im many things but Im not stupid.

She has told them that when we were married I used to show off about knowing better than you lot about the ripper. This is true though isn't it George I did know more than you lot. I am sorry now about what I did and I realise it didn't take brains but I did know more. She has said that I was obsessed with the ripper and used to take cuttings from newspapers and this is true aswell George. I would not say obsessed but I admit that I did have cuttings. I used to read everything about the case. You would of been proud of me.

It is hard to take to have our private life in the papers. The worst of it is she said I used to force myself on her. That will cause me problems in here George. I've told Deafie its not true Ive said I did cut up rough sometimes but I never made her do anything she dint want to. ██████ says I used to go prowling around at night liked to imagine I was Peter Sutcliffe. Its obvious what theyre trying to do George. Theyre trying to make us out like a serial killer "if it bleeds it leads". Its a better story than a pisstaker isn't it. I've never hurt anyone except that copper in that nightclub and Ive done my dues for that long ago. Odd fight here and there but who hasn't.

I am worried that theres lads in here will say Im a rapist theres no difference between a rapist and a kiddyfiddler in here theyre all nonces and its not true about me. I cannot get it out of my head that she came to visit me just for more to tell the papers. And our Jan was in there too saying they thought I was mental because I was going to write to Peter Sutcliffe.

That bit is true and all George. I did talk to them about that. It is true that everyone thinks of my voice when they think of the Yorkshire ripper. We will go down in the annals of history together so I want him to know that I am sorry for impersonating him. I read that they played my tape at the ripper exhibition at blackpool waxworks. I read that Peter Sutcliffe used to go there a lot to look at the exhibitions. He must have heard my voice there. I have spoken to Mr Butler who is our guard on this wing that I want to send this letter and he has said that he does not think it is likely to be allowed. He says he will check and let me know.

Another story they have in the paper is how I was called Sherlock and the lads in the pub bought me a Sherlock Holmes hat because I always said I would have caught the ripper before the police. I don't know where they got that from George but Sherlock is the new nickname along with the others Baggsy and Plastic Jack. Im much happier with that.

Theres a lad three cells down called Pest who gives me the worst bother. Deafie says he s a crackhead Thats probably after your time and all George. Crack is just cocaine smoked in a pipe. It used to just be in London but its been up north for a while now in Leeds and Manchester theres some everywhere truth be told. This lad pest is a wrong un George his eyes are too wide for his head and he says things that make no sense.

I thought he was called pest cause hes a bother but its short for pest controller says deafie. There has been a cockroach problem in our wing George its an old gaol and once theyre in theyre hard to get rid of. This lad pest doesn't mind them tho. Not one bit. Hes got his nickname from eating them. Its sick that isn't it George I told you he was damaged goods but I suppose he doesn't get enough breakfast.

Anyway all the best

Jack

PE8133 HMP Armley, Leeds, 21st April 2006

Dear George,

Now I know that the papers make things up. Its another good reason to tell my story to you and not to anyone else Lord I would never tell it to a paper. This week in ██████ ████████ there is an article telling of the letter peter Sutcliffe wrote to me through the inter-prison postal service. Dear George there is no such thing and no such letter.

Mr Butler came back to me last week to tell me that I needed special permission from my governor and from the other governor. He said that in some cases that might just be a formality but that with me and peter Sutcliffe it would not be allowed because of the fact that the cases are closely linked. He said I could ask for permission if I wanted to but he thought it was unlikely to happen. So I did not send my letter even if I did write it.

It doesn't take Sherlock holmes to work that one out. ████ ████████████ are making up stories. They have made up peter Sutcliffes writing to me. You could have saved those three women John. You have blood on your hands. I was under the influence of voices. What was your excuse John. Drink and drugs I hear. They wrote that he had invited me to see him in broadmoor what use would that be when Im in armley gaol.

It seems to me that if pretending to be peter Sutcliffe is a crime then ████████████ should be locked up. It is even worse than that though George because Mr Butler read this in the newspaper. He said that life will be more difficult for the guards here now because all the prisoners who read ██ ██ will think that one of the screws leaked peter sutcliffes letter to me. He says to watch what I say to people in future.

Deafie says hes not surprised its completely believable. He says theres some decent guards lads who see the man not the crime but that theres as many as that are on the make. How else does so much dodgy stuff go on inside says Deafie. He says it sometimes works for us and sometimes against us and weve got to take the rough with the smooth.

It was a stupid idea George. Lord knows Ive had a few and this one was not a good one and I have learnt how the hard way. I have learnt not to believe papers especially not ████████ and not to believe vikki. I suppose peter Sutcliffe will know all about this anyway he probably reads ████████ everyone does. You cant stop people telling stories George. Perhaps I should tell you my own.

I never wanted to be peter sutcliffes penfriend like they said in ████████ I just wanted to explain myself. I wonder who fooled you the most who you would have disliked the most. I guess Im the one that got away George.

That newspaper has caused me all sorts of problems. I am getting more post now than Ive ever had and most of it is hatemail George. Mr Butler says that there was more. They have to deliver my post to me but they throw out anything too offensive according to some set of rules. Im not sure I'd want to see the stuff that didn't get through George. Ill show some to you now but I wont' be opening anymore.

One more thing George. It is true about pest. Yesterday I saw something I'd rather not. I was walking past pest's cell and he was doing something next to the windowledge. I stopped to see him picking like currants or something out this pile of white powder. He turned around with a cheesy grin and offered one to us. I backed off George. I saw it was flies he had in sugar. Lads not right in the head George its not a good situation.

Your old friend
Jack

John Humble

You think your the Yorkshire ripper? Your not, your a sick, sad little man. I hope you rot in prison for what you done. Your a waste of oxygen.

James Smith

Dear John Humble,

Why would anyone do what you did? Can you imagine the suffering you have caused to the families of those poor murdered girls? What kind of a person could do that? How can you live with yourself? I don't care if you did this last week or thirty years ago, they should lock you up and throw away the key. With any luck you will serve all of your sentence.

Mrs Andrew Howard

I can't bring myself to write your name.

I remember hearing your voice on the TV all those years ago, it still haunts me now. It is inconceivable to me that someone would even think of doing that, of making a recording like that. I don't know what has happened in your life to make you such an angry man but I hope that you will be able to see the error of your ways and apologise to all the people you have hurt. It is the lowest of the low.

Henrietta Morrison

Dear John,

Your crimes are truly terrible but you will be forgiven in the eyes of God if you repent. I pray for your soul and offer you the opportunity of forgiveness. We will remember you at the Sacred Heart. Take heed, my son.

Father Nathan O'Reilly

PE8133 HMP Armley, Leeds, 31st March 2006

Dear Peter,

You probably will not know me but you will know what I did. When the police were looking for you I wrote some letters and sent a tape to George Oldfield saying that it was me who had killed those women. After getting those he thought he was looking for a Geordie because I am from Sunderland.

I hope you will accept my apology for impersonating you. I had no right to do it. It was wrong and I have confessed as much to the police and in court. I am to serve eight years in Armley gaol for perverting the course of justice and it is a fair punishment.

I read that they played my tape at the ripper exhibition at Blackpool waxworks and that you used to be a visitor there. I wonder what you would have thought of that. If you would like to write to me I can be contacted at Armley gaol I am prisoner number 8133. It seems as though we will go down in the annals of history together so perhaps we should be in contact.

Yours respectfully,

Jack the Ripper (aka John Humble)

PE8133 HMP Armley, Leeds, 10th May 2006

Dear George,

Now I am a convicted man I can do some work. Im not that bothered to work but it gets you out the cell gets you money and credit. I have put my name down for whatever comes in. There is a long waiting list so I have also asked to do a course in rehabilitation. Richard says the lass who takes it is fit as a butchers dog Thats what he says George not my words.

You are probably wondering who Richard is. Let me explain Ive got to getting along with Deafie now I know him His real name is Richard McFarlane. I make sure he remembers his hearing aids help him out. Hes teaching me a bit of sign language. Richard used to work in a waste paper factory in Peterlee. Him and his friend Stewie were caught at this lad's flat in Leeds buying five hundred ecstasy pills. Ecstasy was all the rage after you died George all the young lads took them at big parties they made you daft and people liked to hug each other and dance. You and me were always more drinking men I think George. Youd prefer a scrap by the looks of you.

Richard says he didn't do anything wrong except selling pills and he did that for the money. He wishes he knew who it was that grassed him up he has a good idea but he can't be sure. He's a canny lad George does all the courses he can keeps his nose clean except for taking some heroin on his birthday. He says its a treat because its no use taking pills inside he tried it once and he was climbing up the cell walls he says heroins much better inside and easier to get but he doesn't want to be a cunt like all the smackheads so he only does it once a year.

I hope that Richard gets out hes wasting his life in here hes up for release pretty soon so I think he should get out.

Talking to Richard has got me thinking about when I was his age. There was no ecstacy back then George. We used to sniff glue sometimes but it gave you a shocking headache. I preferred cigs and booze. And of course we used to rob things for a laugh.

I remember one day after I left school I was in town down near Durham Book Centre and I turned round the corner and there was this bike just leaning against the railings. a Raleigh chopper looked brand new and I just sat on it to see what it was like when this kid comes out the book centre and says How. That's my bike. So I just pedalled off just to piss him off and he was shouting behind me How. How. Thieving get. Someone stop that lad.

I just pedalled down Durham Road and that was me free I felt like a free bird. I just kept going. Thought to cut onto Chester Road thought about stopping off then thought what my mam would do to us if she found us on a nicked bike. So I kept going and before I knew it I was at Herrington. George that hill nearly killed us but I think the excitement got us through. At Herrington I went for a cruise through the park then found this little road that took us to the A19. I got off the bike and propped it against the bridge and I watched the traffic below.

I started trying to count the cars and when I got to fifty I stopped because it had only taken us about two minutes and it was boring anyway so I started trying to spot the lorries as far away as possible. There was lots of lorries grundfos pumps eddie stobart rumbelows. A roar all the time of all the noise coming and going with the big lorries. Some cars overtaking dead keen to get past but what's the point cause it doesn't make them get anywhere its all going so fast anyway.

I went and sat down in the field by the side of the bridge and watched from there for a bit and I wasnot thinking about that much really just feeling the sound of all the cars and trucks and sitting there and I barely noticed that Id started picking up stones and chucking them down the embankment just watching them roll down the hill. Then I got back up with a handful of stones and climbed back over the fence and onto the bridge and I looked over onto the traffic again and I was like a bomber pilot or something like off a war film looking down onto the enemy targets and dropping me little bombs like ping off the top of a red one and Id hear another ping off the top off a blue one and I was going for number three and I saw a lorry and I tried to get it right on top of the cab and I dropped it a bit late and it hit the back of the lorry and made no sound and then there was a blue car it was like poo sticks really and I hit the blue car on the windscreen and it did a little wobble and a screech and there was marks behind the wheels like black trails on the road like in a film and it pulled in too fast and this gadgey got out and looked at the windscreen and looked back at the bridge and started legging it up the embankment.

I got on the bike and I pedalled off. I was halfway back down the road before he was even up the side of the embankment and laughing so much I wobbled and nearly went over the handlebars but I managed to get straight and kept going and before I got round the corner into some trees I looked back and the gadgey was trudging back down the hill to his car and it wasn't even a close shave.

I dumped the bike in the river at South Hylton didn't want my mam to know so I guess for some people crime does come easy George.

There's only one

Jack the ripper

26 Hawarden Crescent
Sunderland

15th May 2006

Dear John,

I hope you don't mind me writing to you without an invitation to do so. I read about you in the *Echo* and have followed your case since you were arrested. I have written to a number of prison inmates over the last ten years so I have an idea of how lonely "life inside" can be, despite the constant company. I have been led to believe that it can be a relief and a release to have a friend on the outside and I would like to offer you a branch of friendship.

My husband Francis – he was Frank outside the house, of course – was imprisoned briefly. During that time, he said, what he wished for more than anything was a word or two from home, so that he might begin to imagine a world to which he might want to return, a place of hope and possibility. He was denied that outlet and I believe it hurt him greatly. Francis was a very brave man. I presume to hope that by writing to you about our home town I might provide something of an outlet for you.

As you will see from my address above, I too live in Sunderland. I have lived here all my life – my parents moved to Sunderland from Northumberland in the 1930s. I attended the Church High School and went away only briefly, to teacher training college. Have you ever lived anywhere else?

My life now is lived out over an even narrower area as I am rather getting on in years, although yesterday, yearning for some fresh air, I decided to go to Penshaw Monument. I drove, although I find driving very wearying now – it involves such intense concentration. The buses are terribly unreliable and the car gives me a valuable freedom. I parked next to a children's playground, which is a relatively new addition. When was the last time you were at Penshaw, I wonder? It means something to everyone from Sunderland, I am sure, the grand old monument. We have all been there, walked the hill. You see it from the A1 as you pass the Durham turning, and from the train. It is a signal of home.

I am now too old to ascend the hill – my legs just don't have it in them – but the open-cast mine opposite has been freshly landscaped to provide walking trails, a lake and even a kind of grass amphitheatre. I have to say I am ambivalent about most of it – an unused skateboard park, some incoherent sculptures that seem to want to indicate Neolithic stone circles, the obligatory whimsical wildlife silhouettes rendered in cast iron. The amphitheatre, however, I find incredibly satisfying. It seems to me to be in conversation with the monument, a place in which to dramatise great stories about the grand deeds emblematised in that proud structure. It is so often misunderstood as a folly! Nothing foolish here, I can assure you. It was raised by subscription through the freemasons of Sunderland, before that organisation became a silly little club for corrupt policemen and building contractors. It honours the memory of the politician who campaigned for the vote for the working man, Radical Jack Lambton. Imagine a landowner who champions the rights of his employees and tenants? There may be such men in the House of Lords today, John, but if there are they keep their lights well hidden.

It is a copy of the temple of Hephaistos at Delphi in good

Northern gritstone. If Edinburgh is the Athens of the North, Sunderland is its Delphi! So you see; the amphitheatre really is a welcome addition to the site. I can imagine outdoor productions in the summer – "The Birds", perhaps, with the monumental backdrop standing in for cloudcuckooland. Or perhaps Euripides would be better for our locale, something savagely tragic. For I fear that such things will never happen, requiring, as they must, people with generosity of vision in bureaucratic positions.

I must apologise, John. It is most rude of me to go on about my inconsequential day. Perhaps you will write to tell me something of yourself. How is your life in prison? Who are your correspondents? Is there anything you miss that can be posted to you? I would love to read your news, John. I often lack for company and the postman brings me much of mine.

It has been an enjoyable distraction to write this to you. I anticipate yours gladly,

Sincerely,
Freda Jackson

PE8133 HMP Armley, Leeds, 23rd May 2006

Dear George,

I have had a phonecall with Mr Thomas about my appeal. He says the sentence is too severe my age and drinking were not taken into account. He has put all the papers in and now we will wait and see. The phones on the landing are free for legal calls and the guards cant listen in to those. They can listen in to everything else Its up to us to give notice when were on a legal call.

As you know I try to keep my head low I'm not a big one for causing trouble in here. Whenever there are programmes about the Yorkshire ripper everyone watches them and for the week after it has been on I can't lie low anymore Im the most famous man in the wing and people sing at me again. This week there was a programme about my case George.

It was not interested in me though not really theyre interested in anything that makes a good story whether its true or not. I know that now. Lots of moody music and lots of interviews with policemen and an actor to look like me as a young man. He didn't look anything like me George he just looked greasy everyone had a good laugh at that. Theres one journalist from the echo who spent ten year looking for me he was interviewed. Only good bit was that handwriting expert she said I was an enigma. I didn't want to watch this George mainly because the lads in here take the piss something rotten and if you just take that without doing anything your life is a misery. George my life is a misery I don't want to fight Im too old for prison. All the names came out the plastic ripper baggsy jack the twat.

After this programme Pest got onto one with us George. He was saying youre a real cunt baggsy youre worse than a plastic ripper you might as well of killed them yourself Did you want to kill some whores is that what it was all about I reckon you wanted to kill a brasser but you didn't have the bottle. George I just took it but I was thinking this lad is too much if I don't get him off my back he will think he can do anything. but you know the rules George you can't grass in here. I din 't know what to do I was at loss I had a whine to Richard he said nothing just listened and looked radgey.

Next day the news come through that pest's been taken down to segregation for possession. I was made up man George. Later Richard says that's that sorted for you Johnny. I said did you have something to do with that. He says he knows this lad on the twos from wakefield what sells crack. He waited until we were coming back off exercise and ducked into Pests cell hid a rock under his mattress not that well hid but well enough not to fall out. cell check was coming up it wouldn't be long before the guards were doing their rounds Pest would be top of their list. The worst could happen would be that hed find it and smoke it first which would tip him over reckons Richard but he said the plan worked out how hed wanted it best result. I cant believe hes done that for us George hes a friend and ive learnt a lesson.

I suppose I should tell you more about my life growing up. We lived in a brick terrace with an outside netty so did everyone. My dad died when I was seven. We didn't have much after my dad died but it was not a bad life. Plenty to do if you were cunning enough. Used to get into the cinema for free wait for all the kids to come out back doors at the end and sneak in. Hide in the toilets till just before next showing then sneak into screen and lie down beneath the seats near the back. Once it started to fill up you could sit up. Saw some great films that way George Bruce Lee The Way of the dragon Death Race 2000 taxi Driver.

We used to go out robbing like Ive said with lads from the neighbourhood Paul Williams Mike Harding Richard Shuttleworth our Stanley. We used to go out on our bikes too but that all changed when we got interested in music and lasses and drink.

I had three older sisters one younger stepsister think I mentioned them before so there was always lasses around even if none of them wanted anything to do with us. Cora's friends would come round and sometimes they liked to tease me and Stanley. Want to look at our knickers don't you. All that kind of thing. Stanley was too young they thought he was sweet but I did want to look at their knickers George don't we all. Sometimes they'd even show us and then Id get all hot and bothered remember what that was like. I'd need to go and knock one off the wrist sorry to be vulgar George but its true and its something you cant help but think about in prison even when youre fifty odd like me were all animals really.

This one time me and some lads had been playing footie down near Whitburn near where the mill garage was. It must of been a school game on a Saturday morning Havelock juniors because it was that far away we must of been playing whitburn comp or someone like that. I don't remember the game we probably lost we nearly always did but afterwards we were climbing all over this concrete lump by the pitches and one of the techers from the other school came over and asked if we knew what it was we were climbing on we said nah and we werent interested but he telt us anyway. I don't know why I remembered this so well but it stuck in my head maybe because of what happened after but he said it was a sound mirror from the first world war. It was for listening out for ships at sea and balloons like zeppelins I remember that easy enough led zeppelins I thought. He said how they'd put a microphone in front of the concrete and it would focus the sound like a telescope so they could listen at a distance. And then someone said something daft like could you hear one of the nazi sailors letting off and everyone laughed and the teacher just walked away shaking his head. Because it wasn't Nazis in the first world war was it George. I know that now but we were only kids then.

After the game the kids dad that had driven us down in the back of his van took us down the beach to have some chips and we were all running about. This one lad had some bangers he'd brought back from a school trip to france and he was letting them off and chucking them at everyone else and everyone was running in every direction. I ran down the other end of the beach where there's a big cave in the rocks and I was hiding in there right at the back kind of crouching in a corner. While I was hiding this lass come in she was wearing some kind of uniform so she must of just come off work. I was in the back of the cave and watching her and she might of seen me I don't know. She pulled down her knickers and squatted down there in the cave. The stream of piss come out from between her legs between the hair where her minge is. I could hear the bangers going off outside and bouncing around in the cave and there was bangers going of in me too watching her piss. She seemed to piss for so long George and I was hot and bothered I let myself go. She shook her arse when shed finished still squatting and I shook too I trembled George it was just me but she was there. She pulled up her knickers and another banger went off. Fireworks George in that cave. I felt like my first time and it was in a way.

I don't know why Ive told you this George its between me and you no holds barred and its funny what you remember. It might help you understand.

Your Humble friend

Jack

CONVERSATIONS MADE ON THIS PINPHONE
WILL BE RECORDED AND MAY BE LISTENED TO BY
PRISON STAFF. PINPHONES ARE PROVIDED ONLY FOR
USE BY PRISONERS WHO CONSENT TO THIS. IT IS YOUR
RESPONSIBILITY TO ADVISE THE PERSONS YOU SPEAK
TO THAT THE CONVERSATION WILL BE RECORDED AND
MAY BE MONITORED BY PRISON STAFF.

CALLS TO YOUR LEGAL ADVISER, THE SAMARITANS,
CONSULAR OFFICIALS, THE PRISONS OMBUDSMAN AND
THE CRIMINAL CASES REVIEW COMMISSION, OR CALLS
TO CERTAIN OTHER REPUTABLE ORGANISATIONS
ARE REGARDED AS PRIVILEGED AND WILL NOT
BE RECORDED OR MONITORED.

Norris Downing
Ayr

1/6/2006

Dear John,

I know you are not Wearside Jack. I wrote a book about the
Yorkshire Ripper and I know that Peter Sutcliffe was not guilty of all
the murders just as I know you were not guilty of sending the tape.
I know that it has been edited and doctored. I do not yet know who
did this but I will find out. I know you are innocent of the charges
against you for reasons I will explain. I know who really committed
the murders of those women. They will do anything to cover their
tracks and are not afraid to stoop to yet more terrible crimes. I am
determined to stop the real killer from killing again.

I do not know why you have confessed but I have a very good
idea. I know that there are dark forces at work; that they are very
powerful and I know that you have been caught in their snare. Many
innocent people have suffered the same fate as you. You did not do
what you said you have done. How could you? I know what really
happened and I have my suspicions about how this entire thing is
progressing.

I understand how you must be feeling but you should know that
there are those who would help you. Please contact me. I have
information that would finish this for once and for all. You are in a
vulnerable position but it needn't be so.

The real Ripper has got away. I know this because I know who he was. I do not know why this has happened yet but I am assembling my case. The establishment is rotten to the core and there are those who are desperate to make this go away for good. If you share with me what you truly know we will be one step closer. You can trust me: my judgement is clear and I will not stand by injustice.

If you tell me the truth of what happened to you I can help you, John. Trust me, there are good guys out there.

Your friend,

Norris Downing

PE8133 HMP Armley, Leeds, 6th June 2006

Dear Norris,

Mr Downing, I am just writing to put you straight about these letters and the tape sent during the Sutcliffe case. I did send the letters and tape. There was other evidence too and it was correct. My DNA was on the envelope. It is a fact that I did do that. So Mr Downing, you writing to me saying I am not the hoaxer is incorrect but you are correct in saying I am not the killer.

I thank you Mr Downing for saying I am not the killer but I did send the tape and letters and so I am guilty of these charges and so deserve some time in jail but I think eight years was a little too much for these offences. That's why I am appealing against the sentence but not against conviction which I am guilty. I am not really certain what you mean by dark forces Mr Downing, I have been treated well since arrest, you did get that bit wrong Mr Downing.

Anyway it has been nice to get a letter from you and I wish you all the best Mr Downing.

Yours sincerely

John Humble

PE8133 HMP Armley, Leeds, 26th October 2006

Dear George,

There has been talk for some time that a lad on D wing killed himself last week. Something like that gets round Bad news travels faster than good news. Its no surprise that people will talk and the lads on the landing saw the guards panicking They had to run back and get a ligature knife because no one had one on them. It brought back bad memories its better here now but the shock is the same. You feel it George because it reminds you of how crap your life is how some people decide that it is better not to take it anymore. There are all sorts of reactions some lads get angry would you believe that, Angry that someone else has taken the easy way out. It took a couple of days for the noise to get back to normal Lads were more subdued.

Today the notice went up on our landing that someone had taken their own life offering counselling for those affected. He was a troubled soul George this lad He was the one that needed counselling he probably had it and all. They say there will be an investigation but what will they find that he was abused and that he was bullied in prison. Probably what they will find out is that it was not the guards fault it rarely is. Even though this prison was built so that the guards could see everything happening on the wings they have managed to become blind and even deaf to the cell alarms if it suits them. Theyre not all bad just some rotten apples.

Well George my appeal has not been successful. I was called in to the wing office and given the bad news last night. It was heard by the Lord Chief Justice who is the highest judge in the land so that is that. He agreed with judge norman jones. My case was unique and mr Thomass arguments for mitigation did not work because it was so serious what I did George.

Mr Butler told me that I should now think about applying for a transfer to a category C prison. He said a local prison like this was no good for serving another three years. I will listen to his advice George and fill out the forms. I am better now I no longer want a drink. Richard thinks it is a good idea mainly because of the bother with pest. He says because I have not had any relapses through the alcohol they will look favourably at my transfer. He says I should apply to Altcourse near Liverpool he says its a good prison good lads in there lots from the north of England. Theres no category C prisons nearer to sunderland. Not that it matters because none of my family want anything to do with me anymore I might as well be on the isle of wight for all they care.

I will write soon

Jack

PE8133 HMP Armley, Leeds, 5th November 2006

Dear George,

I can hear fireworks outside when I am writing to you. I can sometimes see some rockets exploding in the sky from my cell window. Theres the bars making lines across the view with bright flashes behind. Theres' lines everywhere here George, Wer'e stuck between lines.

Even the exercise yard. Theres no seats and no grass but thats not so bad. Worst thing is theres a net over the top so no proper view of the sky. Theres not a sight of sky you get round here that doesn't have at least one line across it. The nets in the yard are to stop phones and drugs being chucked over the wall so theyre thin nets. You almost don't see them after a while just a little criss-cross in the sky but theyre there getting in the way. The nets inside between the walkways are heavier theyre supposed to catch anyone who falls "was he pushed or did he jump" Im not sure they would. Lads says theyve never seen anyone caught like a fish not that way. normally dangling from a line in here till the guards come round and cut them down.

The yards not bad George. You just walk round in circles with your pals having a natter find out whats been going on and get some fresh air. I tell you what George that is valuable cause of the smell inside. I don't mind it when Im in it but you notice as soon as youre outside its in the stones of the building. sweat dirty clothes crap piss all of it but mainly not a lot of hope.

I have put in my application for a transfer to a category C prison. Keep your fingers crossed George.

Jack

Norris Downing
London, UK

1/11/2006

Dear John,

I am penned in. There are sinister forces at work, John. Murder and extortion; blackmail; threats. It goes all the way to the top. Do not doubt me. The skeins and symbols are there. It all adds up. When the seals are broken.

Now is the time to break their grip John. I urge you in the strongest possible terms to stop being their patsy. They have already done all they can to you. They have ruined your name. They cannot do anymore. Do not let them break your spirit. Name names. Join me and together we will expose the rot in the so-called justice system.

Send word John and I can arrange for someone to visit you and to take your statement. Do not trust the postal service out of prison – they will control your mail and censor your words. I have reason to believe that they have already sent me false mail in your name. It was a poor job, unconvincing. I know your handwriting better than you do yourself and I can smell a fake. Act quickly John. My day will come soon.

Your friend,
Norris Downing

PE8133 HMP Armley, Leeds, 13 November 2006

Dear George,

Mr Horsley QC was right I did take that book from kayll road library. When I give it to the lady she said You taking this out pet. I said Aye. She was fat with glasses she pulled a face I don't know how you can read about this stuff it gives me the willies just thinking about it. I said Aye well it's just a murder-mystery isn't it and I thought its the only way youll be getting the willies love. I guess it takes all sorts she said. She didn't think I was her sort and she was right. She stamped the inside front cover with the date when I'd to bring it back One month, she said Look after it. I tucked it under my arm went out the door onto Kayll Street turned left up towards home and never borrowed another book. I did look after it though george.

Its funny what you remember George. I remember the crem best of all it was like our park the nearest thing we had nearer than barnes park. Remember walking through the crem The sky clear but its bitter cold hands in my jacket pockets with a book dangling from my wrist in a placcy bag I used to have a little bet with myself that I could get across the cemetery without bumping into one of the gadgeys There was a sign saying No person in the Cemetery shall behave in a noisy disorderly or unseemly manner be intoxicated gamble or play any game use improper or indecent language trespass upon any portion of the Cemetery damage destroy or touch any tree shrub plant headstone monument memorial grave or any other property within the Cemetery or obstruct any officer as aforesaid of the Council in the execution of his duty. Must of read that so many times.

near the crem there was cars coming down the drive from Chester Road I cut across the drive there was a hearse coming down the drive the gadgey gives us a look No person shall commit any nuisance within the Cemetery or against any wall or fence belonging thereto I crack on through more gravestones Mary Werre Barry Williams Frances Jackson Donald Carlier Marjorie College I shin up the wall and over onto Helmsdale Road Onto Hadleigh Road Hartford Road Home Me Mam's in the kitchen Is that you Johnny Aye What time's tea She says there'll not be any tea until I get me room tidied She says have you been down the dole Nah library She says there's no use reading books if you've not got a job I say nowt She says You should sign up like our Stanley I said nowt theres not much to say is there shes wrong I shouldn't sign up like Stanley I ignore her and go to my room then come down fifteen minutes later It's liver and mash for tea mam says your dad loved this he loved liver I say It's nice this mam She says Johnny you've got to get yourself a job if you want to eat in this house from now on I cannat afford to feed you anymore You're a man Johnny and you've got to look after yourself You're welcome to stay here but I'll not feed you if you're not earning Alright mam I'll look for work tomorrow Try the building sites They allays need labourers But I've already tried the sites mam they'll not give us anything but mixing cement You can carry a hod can't ya screams me mam You can carry a fucking bag of cement Your head's in the clouds that's your problem Johnny You read too many books you think life's a bloody fairytale Well I'll tell you it's no fairytale raising three bairns on your own on the social It's no fairytale when your husband drops dead at thirty-six It's no fairytale when your other sons in the army getting shot at by micks. Less it Mam Seriously Less it. Don't give me backchat son youre not too old for me to tan your arse Alright Mam I'll get down the dole tomorrow and look for something Me Mam sits down at the table and picks up the Echo I can't see what she's reading but there's an interview with Jimmy Montgomerry on the back Montgommery's retiring Mam says You know when you were a wee babby I went to see that blind feller lives in Silksworth Have you ever heard of him Na Mam He's a fortune teller reads your palm I thought everyone knew about him He told me about you I don't believe in that stuff He said your pa was ganny die young That doesn't mean anything Mam Lots of people die young What he said about you he said you weren't what you seemed I'm not interested Mam I don't believe in that stuff Aye well I do and there's more to life than you'll ever know Eat your liver.

Me Mam curled up on the sofa with a bottle of Teachers on its side on the rug and a Players burnt out in the ashtray The telly doing the closedown noise I say Mam Wake up Mam I give her a shake on the shoulder Johnny Is that you Aye It's bedtime It's past midnight Cora's not back in is she Na Mam Shes a tart that girl She's probably at that Colin's house Aye Mam Come on Get yehself to bed. Johnny Johnny don't leave us You'll never leave us will you Na Mam I'll stay I say I twist the knob on the telly and the closedown noise gans off with a pop I missed you when you were away I lift her up She's a deadweight dead-drunk her feet through her tights smell sharp and malty and I carry her upstairs and put her on her bed She says You're a good lad Johnny and I say Go to sleep Mam It's bedtime and I go to me room and I read them letters again.

I will stop now George I suppose you are probably bored of hearing about my childhood I know I'm bored of writing it. Its the letters and the tape isn't it George They are what is still unsaid. That is why I am here and why I am writing to you again not because I nicked a bike when I was thirteen or a book when I was 15 "I blame the parents". Next time.

John Jack John Jack John Jack John?

GRAPHOLOGICAL ANALYSIS OF WRITING SAMPLE

Analysis of a letter sent to Detective Chief Inspector
George Oldfield, March 1978
Anonymous sample
Writer: Male, DOB unknown, POB probably North of England

A) Form level (legibility, speed, aesthetic qualities, rhythm)
Assessment: Legibility medium to low, speed slow, aesthetics
    spidery, rhythm erratic
Interpretation: suggests anxiety

B) Size of writing
Assessment: Small
Interpretation: Few friendships, applied intelligence

C) Speed
Assessment: Fast
Interpretation: Rushed, panicked, intense

D) Zones
Assessment: Dominant middle-zone
Interpretation: Intense self-involvement, drive to be at the front

E) Baseline
Assessment: Despite lined paper, undulating/erratic

Interpretation: Responsive to outside influence, erratic
personality, stressed, difficulty distinguishing between
reality and fiction?

F) Slant
Assessment: Marked right slant (+3)
Interpretation: Easily carried away, excitable, goal-focused

G) Pressure
Assessment: Heavy pressure
Interpretation: Combined with low standard form this indicates
irrationality and feelings of inadequacy. Pressure heavier
on downstroke: over-ambitious, selfish

H) Spacing
i)   Margins
Assessment: Uneven
Interpretation: Erratic, ambivalent
ii)   Between lines
Assessment: Written on lined paper so fairly even
Interpretation: Inconclusive
iii)   Between words
Assessment: Even
Interpretation: Indicates the writer has consistent
desire for social connection

I) Connections
i)   Connection stroke width
Assessment: Narrow letter, wide connection
Interpretation: Appears relaxed but in reality
uncomfortable with self

ii) **Angularity of connection strokes**
    Assessment: Erratic angularity
    Interpretation: Uncontrolled aggression
iii) Word endings
    Assessment: Angled
    Interpretation: Abrupt, aggressive

I) Specific features of letters
i) **I dot**
    Assessment: Clubbed
    Interpretation: Indicates aggression
ii) **T bar**
    Assessment: Long, right, becoming lighter
    Interpretation: Driven, sarcastic
iii) **D**
    Assessment: Retraced stem
    Interpretation: Independent, shrewd
iv) **Lower loops**
    Assessment: Variety
    Interpretation: Fantasy surrounding the satisfaction
      of desires
v) **Capitals**
    Assessment: Narrow
    Interpretation: Pent-up
vi) **Lower-case**
    Assessment: Pointed tops
    Interpretation: Sharp mind

I) Personal pronoun and signature
Assessment: Personal pronoun lightly left-slanting in contrast
    to slightly right-slanting signature
Interpretation: Conflict between personal and public personas

Conclusions

The writer is highly aggressive and prone to violent outbursts. There is a conflict between his publicly and privately presented personas and he is prone to mood swings. He has problems differentiating between reality and fiction.

Assessment of honesty of writer – there are none of the signs in this sample of what one would expect to indicate that the writer is aiming to deceive.

PE8133 HMP Armley, Leeds, 26th November 2006

Dear George,

This book is what I remembered George This book was like what you might have all the documents all the theories about jack the ripper. I remember seeing the TV version. There was two detectives took you all the way through it through the different lines of inquiry. The prince sleeping with prozzies and getting married in secret. Freemasons hushing it all up. If people do do magic thats how it is isn't it not mind reading or any of that crap its black magic its rituals its making stuff real. I don't believe any of that though George because of them letters. Theyre the real thing not the theories. It doesn't matter what people think thats all make believe. The letters were real words on the page. Blood and Guts. That one with the kidne. This book made us think George it really did. Theres dark things arent there, Things that you don't really want to know about.

It is something else what you can get out of a prison library. Honest to god George theyve got pretty much everything even true crime. Martina Cole, Books on the krays all that sort of thing. Don't tell the papers or theyll stop us having the good books. Ive got two books now George I want to tell you about the first.

Seems everyone knew Id read this book george it was in the mirror after you spoke to the press it was in the book about me I'm Jack. Think the mirror spotted it first the dear boss stuff. Im not so sure you were such a careful reader as that back in the day. "takes one to know one". It is true I was interested in jack the ripper. Its a real life murder mystery not some make believe crap like the Lambton worm. There was a real man who committed those crimes and never got caught.

There's not many that escape justice not many at all but talk to lads in here and youd think it was only the decent ones got caught. Those that do get away with it get all the more famous. If you get caught you're a criminal but if you get away with it you're not. You've won haven't you you've beat the law and if they never find you you've gone somewhere else you're a legend.

This book has the letters in it ones that were sent to the London police in 1888. Theres pictures of the letters so you can see the handwriting. Its neat and tidy not like what youd' imagine for a murderer. Dear boss he was taking the piss wasn't he saying boss. They were't really in charge the police were they cause they couldnt find him. I keep on hearing the police have caught me but they wont fix me just yet. he was pulling they're legs right from the off taking the piss challenging the coppers to find him but they couldn't. Its funny that he didn't care did he he knew they wouldn't get him. I have laughed when they look so clever and talk about being on the right track. He was sending them up again telling them that they got no idea. that joke about leather apron gave me real fits I don't know what the joke he means is must've been something in the newspapers it doesn't say in the book but a leather apron sounds like something out of texas chainsaw massacre. I am down on whores and I shant quit ripping them till I do get buckled. he's down of whores alright he doesn't much like them I guess that bit's why they called him the ripper. Id not read that word buckled before its real history not the shit they taught us in school. Grand work the last job was I gave the lady no time to squeal. He was a sick bastard like but he had them where he wanted them How can they catch me now I love my work and want to start again You don't think hes even talking about murdering prozzies do you its work for him. You will soon hear of me with my funny little games. Funny little games like I says hes sick this lad. I saved some of the proper red stuff in a ginger beer bottle over the last job to write with but it went thick like glue and I cant use it. Thats grim that is something out a horror movie. Red ink is fit enough I hope ha. ha. He just keeps laughing at them its pretty bleak George. The next job I do I shall clip the ladys ears off and send to the police officers just for jolly wouldn't you. The book says that they never found an ear Keep this letter back till I do a bit more work then give it out straight. My knife's so nice and sharp I want to get to work right away if I get a chance. Good Luck. Yours truly. I'm truly yours too George. Jack the Ripper Dont mind me giving the trade name PS Wasnt good enough to post this before I got all the red ink off my hands curse it No luck yet. They say I'm a doctor now. ha ha

It's his words right there on the page. He was the one what wrote that they all think so even the police back then. But he was never caught. He's laughing at them. Haha. He's in fits. It's evil alright all that about the red stuff and lady's ears but he was never caught was he. He's a legend isn't he. No matter how many true theories none of them are going to catch him now not even if they found some DNA.

Reading them letters changed my head. I've never read nothing like that nothing that just sits there and works like that. I could hear his voice like it was me In my head. It was a kind of brainwashing whatever you call it like he was reading them just to me because he was never found was he and that's part of it. He was never found he's just gone and no ones's going find him now no matter what theories they've got. No one's going to know for sure he's immortal he's beyond the grave. he's done something so big and it might have been evil but it wasn't just evil it was something else. and what about that joke he's funny that's the weird thing he's got a sense of humour. The trade name he says that's good. and he's laughing at the coppers The words he uses like he says fits in fits I'm in fits. I like that its funny it doesn't seem so bad to me.

It had to be him what wrote the letter didn't it. He was the only one knew enough they say maybe the second dear boss letter wasn't him that's what it said in that book anyway. some said that he could of read it in the papers and done the second dear boss letter but the first one that's him for sure No way it's anyone else what with the ear the way he says he's going to cut off a tart's ear and then he does it that seems like evidence to me. There's more than just the blood it was written in. It's dark isn't it you have to remind yourself that it' not right that it's more than letters there's murders too people but they were whores weren't they. Im not saying they should of died just that they were whores weren't they. you don't expect the handwriting to be neat you don't expect him to write like that you expect it to be more crazy and messier but then I suppose I'm saying that maybe it's not him maybe they're fakes after all.

This evening in association Mr Butler asked us to get down to the showers. You stink humble was what he actually said but I don't like to make him look bad George. When I got into the shower block there was pest doing something with a razor

I said how man pest what are you doing and he turns around and hes got all blood dripping out his eyes. George I nearly shit myself please excuse my language but it was horrifying made us feel sick. I couldn t budge glued to the spot just watching him. he was ranting at me stuff out the bible like the blood is the life my lord and master save my soul all that. Some other lads come in to see what the fuss was about and hes talking about the blood of the medium even madder stuff. He kept saying I'm no lunatic and all I was thinking was right you are pal just shift over there and I'll be away. Someone must have told mr butler or hit an alarm because three guards come rushing in with ligature knives must of thought the worst. When they saw pest they realised it wasn't that kind of emergency and put down their knives and started talking to him all gently please put down the razor saying please come here Rennie its all right youve hurt yourself lets go and see the doctor. Pest liked that please doctor please doctor I am sane and earnest the sake of the almighty. They took him away quietly to the hospital wing to get him cleaned up. He is not a well man George I expect he will now be transferred but it is probably better for me.

Yours truly

Jack the Ripper

PE8133 HMP Armley, Leeds, 4th December 2006

Dear George,

That lass Helen Rytka. Seeing all about that on the telly. Reading about that in the papers. Near the cattle market. Near the slaughterhouse. That was a horrific place to die that was a timber yard. In between planks of wood and it took you days to find her body. And there you were saying you were left with the picture that you were looking for someone who was mentally ill. Its an odd thought you said there'll be sociologists psychologists and all that lot writing books and lecturing about this. Crime of the century you said. They were talking about how he was going to go for the alltime record in the papers. And they were even saying it in the papers that they were only whores anyway. You weren't disagreeing were you you were saying aye but he was killing good girls and all.

The sun the mirror and the echo George it was always the sun the mirror and the echo. Sun casts the longest shadow but the mirror and the echo tell the best story. I wrote it down on normal writing paper just leaning a bit to the side pen probably just a bic biro lying around I didn't get anything special for it. I did a practice run George oh yes there was copies. I know that people would of liked to see the copies thats evidence that isn't it George but I disposed of that in the bin. I wrote your address on the envelope and I put it in. I did the whole thing in gloves George. Have you ever put a letter in an envelope in gloves you feel daft. But I wasn't going to get caught for fingerprints George and you lot had all mine plenty of times. You were always getting me to stick my fingers in ink just press down here sir and round there thank you sir.

I licked the envelope and I stuck it shut. There wont be anyone who does that now will there only the most stupid. Youd use a flannel or something now. I would of if I'd known what I know now. I walked round to ford post office and put it in the post box there. It wasn't the nearest to me there's a post box on Halsted Square but I wasn't daft I didn't want you to have too many clues. Turns out you cant tell which post box a letter comes from so I didn't need to do that but you never know.

Id taken care George Judge Jones was right. Id read all the papers George been following it on the papers and on the telly for a year ever since they started talking about a new ripper. Seen the crap photofits read about you saying he was a sly bastard not to get caught so far You didn't know what was going on George it was pitiful. I was polite and all George. Do you want to read your letter again. I think you do. Im not proud of what I did George but the writing cant of been bad can it now.

Dear Sir,

I am sorry I cannot give my name for obvious reasons I am the ripper. Ive been dubbed a maniac by the press but not by you You call me clever and I am. You and your mates havent a clue That photo in the paper gave me fits and that lot about killing myself no chance Ive got things to do, My purpose to rid the streets of them sluts. my one regret his that young lassie Mcdonald did not know cause changed routine that nite, Up to number 8 now you say 7 but remember Preston 75, Get about you know, you were right I travel a bit You probably look for me in Sunderland don't bother I am not daft just posted letter there on one of my trips. Not a bad place compared with Chapeltown and Manningham and other placesWarn whores to keep off streets cause I feel it coming on again, Sorry about young lassie.

Yours respectfully

Jack the Ripper

Might write again later I not sure last one really deserved it. Whores getting younger each time. Old slut next time I hope, Huddesfield never again too small close call last one.

George it wasn't hard to write like that but I must have done a decent job. I had read all the papers George and the dear boss letters. I copied them out wrote down some of the choicest phrases. I couldn't get those letters out my head to be honest George, I had to do something about them. I couldn't stop thinking about them I wanted to prove it. I wanted to show you what for. It was me I needed you to hear me my voice his voice. You'd got it all wrong hadnt you you did'nt know what you were doing you were looking for him everywhere. the papers were the worst they just made things up. They didn't know the story of jack proper how could they call him a ripper he wasn't that was he. I never even knew any whores myself never went with any. What did I have against whores how could I write them words. They just come out it wasn't like I planned them I just read the first letters didn't I and I thought I knew how he talked or how he wrote anyway and I thought I could do that.

I wanted to be better than I was than people thought I was. I was better than that I knew I was. I had a gift I could do his voice me in his voice. I knew him better then himself really and no one knew me. Never really talked to me never really asked me what I thought. Of course in the pub you know all the lads would chat and that but not really listen. I was always the quiet one. So I spoke out I always thought I could of been a writer well I am aren't I. I can't help myself can't stop writing now even in my head.

This is my story.
Jackanory

PE8133 HMP Armley, Leeds, 7th December 2006

Dear George,

I keep getting off the point in my letters to you. I am sorry about that George there is quite a lot to think about and everything comes crowding in at once. I know you will understand that it is quite hard sometimes to see the wood for the trees I think it must be the same for everyone. I know that you didn't always manage it. I suppose it is something that people can learn how to do but there is so much noise isn't there George. Theres everything in the papers everything on telly everything in books everything you hear on the phone. Its a miracle really that we don't all go a bit mad George with all the stuff that goes through our minds.

As it was said by mr horsley at my trial I had read about Joan Harrison in the papers and you were misled by that. It was in the mail it was just a story I read. I read the papers everyday after writing to you. Everyday across the crem to kayll road library hopping over the walls walking past the daffodils sitting down there going through the papers. I had nothing better to do. The sun the mirror and the echo. Not a peep George not a whisper. The sun did this story all about how it was like a film set. Theyve always been sick bastards them right George. I wrote the mirror next because their Close ups was always on about the ripper they knew what was going on. I got the address off the paper and wrote the dialling code to throw you off the scent. That was a good one wasn't it George. I told them how much I respected you George Im not sure you ever believed that really but it was true I was worried for you and all.

Thought the mirror needed a shove George I wanted to see my words in the mirror. Had a go at seeing the future and that turned out better than expected didn't it.

I sometimes wonder if I somehow knew but then I know that is a daft idea. I have to remind myself I don't believe in that rubbish.

You know the letter to the mirror George but its worth repeating.

Dear sir.

I have already written Chief constable, Oldfield "a man I respect" concerning the recent Ripper murders. I told him and I am telling you to warn them whores I ll strike again and soon when heat cools off. About the Mcdonald lassie, I did nt know that she was decent and I am sorry I changed my routine that night, Up to murder 8 now You say 7 but remember Preston 75. Easy picking them up dont even have to try, you think theyre learn but they dont Most are young lassies, next time try older one I hope. Police havent a clue yet and I dont leave any I am very clever and dont think of looking for any finger-prints cause there arent any and dont look for me up in Sunderland cause I not stupid just passed through the place not a bad place compared with Chapeltown and Manningham cant walk the streets for them whore, Dont forget warn them I feel it coming on again if I get the chance. Sorry about lassie I didnt know.

Yours respectfully

Jack the Ripper

Might write again after another ones' gone. Maybe Liverpool or even Manchester again, to hot here in Yorkshire, Bye.

I have given advance warning so its yours and their's fault.

The Yorkshire Ripper Letters

From pp 377–87 of *Texte zu Theorie und Praxis forensischer Linguistik* 1990.

This writer, then, was thoroughly functionally literate in the sense that he could perfectly well express himself in writing but really rather illiterate in terms of his ability, or perhaps one should rather say inclination, to conform to the accepted standards of written style. The letters were all written on sheets taken from pads of lined paper, no doubt with a ballpen. The first two occupied two pages each. There were no margins and no paragraphs though each contained a postscript, designated as such in only one case. The handwriting was adequately legible for the most part but frequently clumsily executed. The punctuation was well below the standard that one would hope that Ordinary Level examination candidates achieve. It was very often difficult to judge whether a particular mark on the paper was meant as a full-stop or a comma (or even had any significance!) but there certainly weren't enough of either by the ordinary canons. About a third of the sentences had no full-stop. About a third began without a capital letter, but initial capitals regularly appeared on names (though not internally in McDonald) and the pronoun *I* was always capitalised.

Of the three opening salutations, two had full-stops, rather than the conventional comma, and the third was unpunctuated. The placing of apostrophes, where they were bothered with at all, was highly erratic. No use was made of exclamation or question marks (the latter orthodoxly requisite in only two places) or of parentheses, though there was one use of what is in fact apparently (among schoolchildren at least) quite a common so-to-speak punctuational folk usage by which inverted commas (quotation marks) are employed as parentheses. These occurred around *a man I respect* at the beginning of Letter 2. At the one place where quotation marks were requisite they were not employed. What was very notably idiosyncratic was the frequent tendency to leave a space before completing a contracted spelling with its final *nt* etc.

The spelling seemed to suggest perhaps rather a contemptuous attitude to orthodox orthography rather than just incompetence. The forms *nite* and *cause* (used five times with no use of the ordinary spelling *because*) are obviously simply defiance of orthodox usage. So also maybe were to some extent *I not* for *I'm not* (twice) and even possibly *they're learn* for *they'll learn* and *to hot* for *too hot* (which last was spelt correctly on another occasion). All of these last three could read back as perfectly normal spoken forms in the English of a speaker of the sort heard on the tape. Indeed, only the weakening to a schwa vowel of the adverb *too* (in the way general English treats the preposition *to*) is confined to Northern English dialect among these usages. The extra *s* in *obviously*, the superfluous *h* in *my one regret his*, the missing *r* from *Huddesfield*, the missing final *s* from *them whore*, the missing word *is* from between *My purpose* and *to rid* and the failure to use initial capital on Ripper at one point were all no doubt merely slips.

The literary style was in general an unremarkable clumsy mixture of colloquialisms, dialectalisms, slang, telegraphese and journalese but it did contain some strikingly idiosyncratic items.

PE8133 HMP Armley, Leeds, 24th December 2006

Dear George,

I have wrote to you about one book. The other one is this book of horror stories. It has this story in it thats about jack the ripper too. I think you will enjoy the whole thing here see what you think happy Christmas.

John

YOURS SINCERELY, JACK THE RIPPER

I met him in a sleazy bar in the Roppongi district. He looked uncomfortable and out of place in his smart lounge suit. Off-duty marines fist-pumped and bear-hugged at the bar while this old stuffed bird perched on his stool sipping a drink.

"Dr Black?" I asked.

"You must be John Carver," he replied. We shook hands. I was surprised by the firmness of his grip. I had expected something more effete.

I went straight to the point. "This doesn't seem like your type of a place, doctor. I can't help but wonder why we're meeting here."

"You're quite correct, Mr Carver," he sighed. "This is not my sort of a place at all. But I'm afraid my investigations have led me to many places that are not at all my sort of a place. We could have met at the Imperial but our work would have necessitated a trip to Roppongi sooner or later."

"You seem to be getting a little previous there, doctor. Our work? I'm just here for a drink, buddy. And I'm happy drinking alone if it saves me a little work."

He shuffled uncomfortably on his bar stool. I guessed this guy wasn't used to being slapped down. "I apologise, Mr Carver. I have rather jumped the gun. But I am hoping to interest you in my enterprise."

"Okay, doctor, but let's take it one step at a time. I'm going to need to quench my thirst before we get to talking about any enterprises."

The smile returned to his face. "Once more, I apologise. In my eagerness to meet you I have quite forgotten my manners. What can I get you?"

"A Bloody Mary, heavy on the Tabasco."

"Certainly."

I gave him the once over while he ordered the drinks. He was a textbook British gent: quality tailoring, Savile Row. He was around sixty and in pretty good shape for his age. He'd contacted me through the agency website, said he was a crime writer and had a case he needed help with. He'd been vague about the details.

He passed over my drink and raised his own glass. "Campai!"

"Campai, doc." With satisfaction I felt the burn of the Tabasco on my lips. Just the way I like it. "So Dr Black, a little more information a little less action, please."

"Very droll, Mr Carver. Please, call me Marius." He paused, and fixed me with a squint look. "You have, I take it, heard of Jack the Ripper."

"Come now, Marius." I gave him the stink eye. "What do you take me for? Of course I've heard of Jack the Ripper. Who hasn't? Saucy Jack, the original Psycho, the daddy of all serial killers. He killed, what was it, five prostitutes? Gutted them like fish, right?"

"Well, that's one way of putting it. He eviscerated his victims, yes, but not without a certain intent. He removed parts of the reproductive apparatus from some of the women. Others he butchered in a more savage and frenzied fashion. This all took place in a short period in the autumn of 1888 in Whitechapel. And then he disappeared."

I saw it right then, the dense sparkle of obsession in his eye. This man was a believer. "Okay, so you've got the facts. But why are you laying them on a private eye in a Tokyo dive?"

He looked up at me from the rim of his glass. "I admire your candid approach, Mr Carver. May I be frank with you?"

"Certainly, doc," I smiled, "as long as I can be Ernest with you."
I winked at him.

He guffawed, a cartoon English toff. "You may indeed, John.
You may indeed." He paused and glanced around him, scanning
the room for eavesdroppers. He dropped his voice. "Have you read
about the hostess killings?"

I nearly choked on my Bloody Mary. This was close to home.
Three Western girls working in hostess bars had been brutally
murdered in the past three weeks. The police were keeping the
details to themselves but the rumours were working their way
through my network regardless. Each girl had been slashed right
open and left to die where they fell. Each had been found down an
alley in Roppongi or Shibuya. The word on the street was that this
was some kind of Samurai complex gone wrong: ritual seppuku
meted out on foreign working girls. The last girl found had been one
of my clients.

"It's been difficult to miss, Marius. Top of all the news bulletins.
Our very own ronin nightcrawler."

"Indeed," he replied. "Well, I'm here to test out a theory."

"Theorise away, doc." I couldn't say I wasn't interested.

He cleared his throat. "As you obviously know, the most notori-
ous thing about Jack the Ripper is the fact that he was never caught.
His evasion of justice has left something of a vacuum that has been
filled by ever more salacious rumour and speculation. Perhaps the
killer committed suicide. Perhaps the killer was a woman. Perhaps
the killer fled Britain. Perhaps there was more than one killer, a team.
Perhaps the series of murders was orchestrated, ritually, a
Freemasonic conspiracy. Many figures have been implicated. The
painter Walter Sickert. The Royal Surgeon William Withey Gull. Even
the Prince regent himself."

I jumped in. "I've heard the stories, doc." He was getting carried
away and would run all night if I didn't reign in his obsession. "I'm

still no wiser about what this has to do with me or why you're even in Tokyo?"

"Well, Mr Carver, my theory will explain all that, but it is rather difficult to swallow. I believe, no, in fact, I am certain that the killer who claimed the lives of those poor women in Whitechapel is also responsible for the hostess murders."

"Hold it right there, doc," I spluttered. "You are aware that this is 2025, right? That was 150 years ago?"

He looked at me with a burning intensity. "I am all too aware of the date, Mr Carver. I have become very interested in dates."

"Tell me more," I urged.

"I want you to know, John, that I am no amateur Ripper obsessive, no crackpot pervert with a groupie's yearning to cosy up to the killer—"

"You don't look the type," I told him, but in truth, I thought, he looked exactly the type.

"It started as a book project, but it grew once I got deeper into the research." He was becoming animated, motioning with his hands.

"I could sense a pattern. I don't have a lot of truck with astrology, Mr Carver, or indeed numerology. I've been working with the Tarot and theoretical physics. All seventy-eight Tarot cards can be identified with the seventy-eight dimensions of the F6 Lie algebra of the E4-E5-F6 physics model. This has led me to certain conclusions about the system the killer has been using. It fits with the kind of occult ritual prominent in London at the end of the nineteenth century. Theosophy was the main mover, of course, and I've found a few old records referring to a splinter-group from the first Lodge of the Theosophical Society established in London that was dedicated to more intense occult study. It seems they operated from a room above the Viaduct Tavern in Newgate Street, before disintegrating in early 1887. Differences of interests, naturally. The majority of the group were fascinated by the occult possibilities of the Platonic solids and Chaldean writings; one renegade was becoming obsessed with medieval demonology. Clearly, he hadn't read the Faust legend—"

"Or maybe he had read it, Marius. Maybe he'd read it very closely. But you still haven't come to the crunch. Why are we here?"

He removed his glasses and wiped the lenses with a monogrammed handkerchief as he delivered his final assessment, carefully and deliberately.

"As I said, John, I have had some joy with my system. The pattern is unmistakeable. There is a repetitive date sequence and the locations shift in accordance with the Chinese zodiac."

"The locations? I'm sorry doc, you've lost me there."

"Moscow 1913. Chicago 1955. Nairobi 1983. Bangkok 2014. And now Tokyo 2025."

"Sounds like the Olympics."

"If the Olympics were a sick travesty of misogynistic, occult murder, then you might have a point, John." He eyed me with disgust. "This is serious man! There are lives at stake."

I wasn't going to be railroaded so easily. "You're doing it again, Dr Black. I'm afraid you're getting ahead of yourself. You expect me to believe that Jack the Ripper is some kind of time-travelling, globe-trotting magician?"

"A mage? An occult experimentalist who has discovered the darkest of secrets – those of human sacrifice and immortality? Indeed he is: a black magician, a sorcerer."

I finished my drink and made to go. "Well, doctor, it's been nice meeting you but I guess you must be getting late for your appointment with your shrink—"

He looked downcast. "I thought you were a professional," he muttered. "I can pay."

Now he was talking my language. I settled back onto my stool. "100,000 yen buys you my attention for another couple of hours."

"Then we have no time to lose," he said. "Follow me."

He jumped off his stool like a man half his age and made straight for the door, past the marines who were putting on an impromptu performance of fire-breathing, taking it in turns to spray flames from their mouths. I checked myself in a mirror behind the bar, gave myself a wink, and followed him out.

2.

By the time I caught up with him enough to talk he was halfway to Nishi-Azabu. This guy was like a stinger missile, autoguided towards his target. "Hey, Dr Black!" I called after him. He just kept on going.

I jogged up alongside and saw the grim set of his face. "What's the hurry?"

"There is no time to waste. If my calculations are correct, and I believe that they are, it could happen at any time."

"Calculations?" I asked. "You're going to have to slow down, doctor, and I don't mean the way you're walking. I've never had much of a head for maths. I'm more of a lowly cleaner."

"Of course." He was breathless and impatient. "Such is the noble art of detection. In fact, I wasn't much of a mathematician before I stumbled across this material. All that matters is that we need to get to the Man Time hostess bar as soon as we can. It's just around this corner..."

He marched on like a man possessed while I trailed in his wake. Perhaps, I thought, when we get there he might cut us enough slack to catch our breath.

Standing beneath the neon sign, a blinking stickman in a suit, the doorman, a standard-issue Yakuza goon, nodded us inside. Dr Black checked in his coat. I preferred to keep mine in case I needed to make a quick exit. The Mama-san did the bowing and kowtowing and ushered us into a booth. We were joined immediately by two hostesses: a curvy bottle-blonde in a red kimono and a breathtaking sister head-to-toe in black. I had to credit the good doctor; he'd picked a peach of an establishment.

"Good evening, gentlemen," purred the blonde. "I'm Amanda and this is Joy. What can we get you to drink?" No disguising her Englishness beneath a mid-Atlantic twang; an old family and an expensive education, holidays in Cape Cod. Dr Black took a mineral water – the guy meant business now. Amanda went to get the drinks and Joy – African, probably West Coast – gently quizzed me about my favourite topic – me.

Just as I was getting comfortable, Black interrupted. "Look over there, John. That Salaryman. What do you make of him?"

I followed the doctor's eyes to an elderly Japanese Joe wearing thick, milk-bottle glasses. He looked as dangerous as a marsh-mallow machine-gun: his suit was creased and his shoes scuffed. His face was red with the Scotch on the table and he had his arm around an Eastern European-looking broad. "Mid-ranking bureaucrat, interior ministry," I said. "His wife is the boss and this is his downtime."

"How do you know Tanaka-san?" asked Joy, looking at me in awe like I'd just solved the mystery of dark matter.

"Lucky guess. What's his story, Joy?"

"Tanaka-san is a very sad man," she said, feeling every word. "He likes to come here because his home is not a happy home. His wife says he is a disappointment to her. His father-in-law is a very big man, very powerful man. Tanaka-san is not really a man at all."

"And who is that with him?" asked Black.

"That is Ola," said Joy. "Ola looks after Tanaka-san. Ola is his mama." Joy chuckled, a rich gurgling chuckle.

"Let's straighten this all out, doc. Not that I'm not delighted to be sharing a booth with wonder and Joy, here…" – she chuckled again, and slid a bit closer on the seat – "but I'm still playing catch up on what exactly we're doing."

He looked shifty, like he didn't want to spill his guts in company. Amanda returned with our order and sat down next to the doctor. "My calculations are interesting in that they yield very specific information," he explained. "The next, erm, event..." – he looked nervously at the ladies – "will take place within a few hours and within a short distance of this precise location. I cross-referenced my research with the digimaps and this is the most likely starting point for our investigation, the Man Time hostess bar."

Amanda perked up. "Gosh, how exciting this all sounds. Are you policemen?"

I creased up. "You wouldn't catch me wearing a badge, Mandy. I prefer to work alone."

"So you're an investigator?"

"Something like that."

"And you, doctor?"

"I'm a researcher. But I also need to speak to you very seriously. I have reason to believe that you are in great danger and I need to know as much about the patrons and employees of this bar as possible, in order to protect you."

Amanda smiled, an elegant and knowing smile, the smile of a woman used to being underestimated. "I take it you're referring to the hostess murders? Well, we're quite well protected as it is, Dr Black. You may have noticed Haruki on your way in? I believe it would take a particularly brave man to get past Haruki and his collection of knives."

I felt an involuntary shiver race down my spine. "But you don't understand me!" The doctor was flustered now. "It probably won't happen here, but after you leave, on your way home. It could be any one of you. And it could be any one of these men from whom you are at risk."

Once again, Mandy flashed that smile. "I don't know what you think is going to happen to us, doctor, but I assure you that Joy and

I are really quite streetwise. You have to be in this business." At this, Joy slid her hand along her thigh, raising the hem of her kimono. The doctor looked like he was about to explode. The glint of a pearl-handled revolver tucked into her garter mirrored Joy's knockout smile.

"But you still don't seem reassured," continued Mandy. "So let me introduce you to our clientele. That is Tanaka-san."

"The gentlemen know Tanaka-san already," interrupted Joy. "He's a sad, sad man," she clucked.

"Joy is quite right," continued Mandy. "Tanaka-san is a pathetic man. I am under no illusions that anyone can be dangerous in the wrong circumstances, but I am also as certain as can be that we will order a taxi home for Tanaka-san shortly after he drinks his fourth whisky. If he is home later than 10 p.m. his wife becomes suspicious and his father-in-law will make his life a greater misery than it already is."

"What about that chap there?" asked Black, pointing to a large-bellied, Saturnine young man in a hooded top.

"Nick?" asked Joy. "Nick is a lovely boy, with a big heart. He is too rude, though! Tonight he is here to see Keeshor. Keeshor has something from Nepal for Nick."

"What?" blustered the doc. "Some kind of magical artefact? An ancient text?"

The girls laughed. Mandy raised her thumb and forefinger pinched together to her mouth, inhaled deeply and went cross-eyed. "Keeshor has a sideline. Maybe you guys want some? You could do with loosening up a little."

There was one man left in the place we hadn't discussed. In a booth by the corner, an aging gaijin in an elegantly tailored suit, entranced by his conversation with a young Japanese hostess. We all looked at once and the mood shifted subtly.

"I don't know who that is," said Mandy lightly.

"He is new here," added Joy.

"That's our man," concluded Black.

3.

It was 2 a.m. before our man set to leave. I'd enjoyed our time with Mandy, Joy and later Miwako, briefly, and even Mama-san, but Black had taken a turn for the worse. Tanaka had got drunk on his fourth whisky and his cab had been called, as Mandy had predicted, and Black had ordered a whisky of his own. Nick had disappeared into a back room with Keeshor, re-emerged with a benevolent smile on his face and slipped out of the joint: Black became morose and sunk another two whiskies. Only our friend, Dr Black and I were still standing and it seemed unlikely Black would manage that for long.

Mandy had accepted a spying mission to the suit corner. The intelligence gathered was inconclusive. His name was Aickman. He was a Scot, working for a Chaos Fund in the Time Tower. Mandy said he didn't seem the type to her and that was good enough for me, but Dr Black wanted to be sure. When Aickman settled his bill and left we followed sharp on his tail, tipping the girls and heading down the stairs. As we passed Haruki, I slipped him a 10,000. "Hey, big man. Any idea where the suit's headed?" Haruki bowed and grunted. "Kapuseru." The capsule hotel just off Gaien-Higashi-Dori. It always paid in my game to keep the organised crime guys sweet.

We tailed Aickman a couple of blocks, holding just far enough behind. Black got majorly excited when he paused next to a pair of party girls, all chromataphoric leg-warmers and bikinis, gurgling to me about this being it. But Aickman just fired up a nicostik. Sure enough, the trail went dead a block later when he walked into the well-lit lobby of capsule hotel, clouded the creds and slid into a pod.

Black started rambling and I walked alongside.

"Don't understand it. Double-checked the equations. Nowhere

else like that on the digimap. It was the magus. Had to be! Can't understand it at all."

We were wandering aimlessly back towards Roppongi Hills. I led us down a little short cut I knew, off the main roads. A swirling fog was creeping in, a real pea-souper.

"Don't beat yourself up, doc," I reassured him. "You weren't so far off the mark."

"What do you mean, John?" he slurred. "You've humoured me long enough. There is no killer. I'm just a sad, obsessive old hack."

He stumbled and I caught him with my left arm. With my right I reached inside my coat and felt the sharp steel of my blade. I pulled it clear of the sheath with one clean motion.

"I wouldn't say that, doc," I said, as I raised the blade before his goggling eyes. I brought it down across his gut in a slick stroke. "And there's no need to call me John anymore, buddy. I'm Jack."

© Robert Blake, 1949

26 Hawarden Crescent
Sunderland

26th December 2006

Dear John,

I hope you will not mind me writing again. I realise that receiving
mail from a stranger may elicit quite an ambivalent response and I am
concerned not to make any assumptions about your reasons for not
replying. I would like sincerely to reassure you that should you want
me not to write any further I will put down my pen upon notice of
your wishes. I have no desire to impose myself where I'm not wanted!
Please just let me know by return of mail and I shall cease my
scribbling.

I have just passed a very lovely Christmas Day with my grand-
children – I have three, Jennifer, 4, Charles, 7, and Robert, 9 – and
now I am back home my thoughts have turned to my friends in
prison. I know this is a particularly lonely time of year if you are
unable to see friends and family. I hope you have managed to find
some modicum of festive cheer!

The curious thing is that I am not entirely a stranger. I should have
mentioned this in my first letter though I did not want to trouble you
with something that seems really rather insignificant in the grand scheme
of things. I was your Sunday School teacher briefly in the mid-sixties.

I don't suppose you will remember but your mother brought you to church for a period and I think she found some solace there, although I do not know why she stopped attending. Faith is such a personal thing, John. I remember a bright young boy. You took care of your younger brother – I am afraid I cannot for the life of me recall his name – sitting him next to you and answering questions on his behalf. I remember you took great delight in the stories we read, but I am sad to say that my memory fails to reach any further towards specifics.

I did not mention this in my first letter because I did not want to oblige you to respond. I realise how disingenuous it must seem that I write this now, in my second letter, when you have not responded to my first. How have my motives changed in the intervening time? How does this not recapitulate the imposition of some kind of debt? In short, I have reconsidered. I do not think you will feel any obligation and I do not intend to impose any. I feel, in retrospect, that it was not entirely honest of me not to admit to my personal interest, and so I hope to correct that sin of omission.

I trust that you are settling in now, John. I understand that prison life can be particularly complicated in the earliest months as the prisoner has to learn the ropes and re-acclimatise to a life of captivity, routine and boredom. Many of my earlier correspondents have taken up hobbies to pass the time and to have something to focus on. One friend, James, took up playing bridge, for which he was roundly mocked – it is such a middle-class game, is it not? Not quite what is expected of a guest at Her Majesty's Pleasure. But he recognised that it offered a lifetime's opportunity for improvement, that he could play it again and again and never play quite the same game. He persisted, despite the taunts – he had, of course, a handful of colleagues in this – one can play without a full hand but it's not the same – and he still plays now, on the outside, is a member of a club and writes a column for a magazine on the subject. How wonderful! New skills hard won are not so easily lost.

My own longstanding hobby is calligraphy. I have never progressed beyond the level of hobbyist, although I have been urged to take it further. I am quite content in the pleasure it gives me as I practice it and I fear that professionalising the skill would take a great deal of the enjoyment out of it – deadlines and suchlike. I took it up when Francis died. I was looking for something to do that would also find me company. I was, for many years, an art teacher, so I knew I would have some basic proficiency in terms of control of the pen and the stroke. Sunderland University, as you may or may not know, John, has an excellent school of art and design and within that a number of teachers who specialise in calligraphy. I was fortunate enough to study under Professor Clayton when he was a visiting lecturer at the St Peter's campus and his gift for instruction was remarkable. He would take us on field trips to St Peter's church, on the site of the St Peter's monastery, home of the monks of Monkwearmouth. This was not far to venture into the field, if the truth be told – just across the road – but it was an inspired thing to do. There, in the peace of the church, he would talk about the monastery and spirituality and ask us to imagine the craft of writing in this light – and it was light, John, multi-coloured light that poured through the stained glass windows. There, amidst council built tower-blocks, this little oasis remains. I confess that at first I found the tower-blocks depressing – a pair of sixties monoliths, overshadowing this ancient site. But as time has worn on I have warmed to them. It seems appropriate that these homes provided by the community of Sunderland for the community of Sunderland should be where they are, near to this holy site. I have begun to enjoy the juxtaposition of modern and ancient. They *do* talk to each other but they converse in a language we must strain to understand.

I think it a wonder, John, that we walk the same ground that our ancestors walked, that history persists. Time does not feel very linear to me, in my dotage. It seems to swirl. Sometimes, the stories I read are as real as my own memories – sometimes, perhaps, yet more real! Certainly, at Monkswearmouth, history feels very present. Did you know that the seventh-century founder of St Peter's, Benedict Biscop, brought French glass workers and stone masons to build his monastery and they founded craft communities on the banks of the Wear? To think that Sunderland was a centre of medieval learning and book production, of construction and illumination, a thriving home to craftspeople and innovators in the written word and the material of life – the Silicon Valley of its day, perhaps?

Did you know, John, that illuminated texts produced in the scriptorium at St Peter's were in such high demand that the monks developed a new minuscule script that would allow them to write more rapidly and produce books at a higher rate? I suppose – to stretch the Silicon Valley analogy a little too far – the contemporary equivalent would be some form of computer code or an algorithm. This was where Bede grew up, John! It birthed written English!

But I am wittering on. It is a failing, even when I write – perhaps, particularly when I write. You have most likely already put this letter to one side, tired of reading the ramblings of a lonely old lady. The truth is that were I to write about what I spend most of my time doing – scouring my cupboard for teabags I am certain I have bought, worrying about my daughters, listing the numerous pills I now have to take – my letters should be so unutterably dull. I do not care to remind myself in the written word of my day-to-day existence. This is an opportunity to reflect and to remember, to allow thoughts the freedom to roam. I make no excuse for that.

I enclose a sample for you in the insular minuscule script developed in Sunderland. The text is taken from one of the Durham Proverbs, the original manuscript of which is one of the Cathedral's treasures. It translates, roughly, as: "It does no good for all truth to be told nor all wrong imputed." Food for thought, no doubt. I hope it may brighten your cell and remind you of your hometown,

Yours fondly,
Freda

Ne
ðēah eall
sōþ āsǣð
Ne eall
sār ǣtwiten

PE8133 HMP Armley, Leeds, 14th January 2007

Dear George,

So that is that for leeds my transfer has come through. Mr Butler called us down to the guards room and I was thinking I was for the high jump trying to think what Id done wrong. Then he shakes my hand and says congratulations John youre moving along. I didn't know what he meant George at first I thought he was threatening us or something. He just says you don't look very happy. I said what do you mean Im moving along. Youve got your transfer to altcourse he says You need to say your goodbyes and pack your stuff youll be off tomorrow. I have to admit George I had a bit of a cry at that. Mr butler looked embarrassed then he said pull yourself together man its not fit to be crying. Then I started laughing and just said thanks you mr butler thank you very much. He said pull yourself together and get back to your cell Ill see you bright and early tomorrow for transfer.

Ive told Richard. I was careful how I said it because I know hes waiting for his transfer and mines come through first hell be worried about being stuck here now. But he was just happy for us. Thats mint john lad he says thats fucking mint. You need out of this shit hole Its going to be great at Altcourse. I said Id write he said that would be canny.

There wasn't many more I needed to say goodbye to. I looked out for Howie at canteen but I didn't see him. Ill write him from altcourse maybe or maybe not we'll see. George Ill tell you more after the move. Ive not got much to pack just one or two books. Theres not been much chance to earn anything here Im glad to be moving along. I will tell you more from my new home.

I have attached another letter from this woman Freda. I am not sure about her George. I think she is one of these crackpots maybe. You know them women that like to write to famous murderers and that, Ive no idea who she is we never went to church or Sunday school. I think she is after my signature maybe. Its a bit strange that Anyway I am moving along now so she wont be any bother anymore.

Your old friend

Jack

PE8133 HMP Altcourse, Fazakerley, 21st February 2007

Dear George,

Well it is very different here from armley gaol. Its not exactly a holiday camp but it doesn't smell as bad its not as noisy. I don't want to say its not as dangerous because I don't know yet I am sure there are still some angry people in here George. Theyre banged up after all.

It took 3 hours in a van there was a stop for water and pissing and that. Two hours checkout at leeds two hours check in here. First night centre for one night now I am in a 4-man cell with 2 others. There is Buster who was a postie and is about my age. He keeps himself very smart gets down the showers before everyone else in the morning. Buster does the cryptic crosswords and reads a lot and is educating himself while hes inside. He is the staff liason on the wing which means hes the rep for us with the guards. We talk mainly about true crime and murder mysteries and that. He says real detective work is not glamorous like in the films theres no dames and no shoot outs mainly just serving injunctions for divorce and following fat fellers wives around. Busters jewish wears a skull cap on holy days Lads keep trying to get him into fights with the muslims He comes from Birkenhead so most of the lads thinks he fancies himself. Says hes in for non-payment of fines smells like a bit of bullshit to me must have been in six year already.

Tom the Mong reminds me a bit of Richard. Hes another one inside for selling drugs got caught with lots of cocaine and he seems quite proud of that. Toms Chinese but hes from Boro and he talks like someone in a chinkie restaurant in Boro which makes sense cause that's what his mam and dad do. I could tell straightaway that Tom was a ex squaddie. When I met him I said I bet you've been in Afghanistan. He was like how do you know that? I said never you mind son. Everyone takes the piss out of Tom cause hes daft as a brush. His real name is Jun Lee He told us yesterday when we were walking in the yard. His families from gwang zoo province. Theyre my new housemates George and were getting along just fine.

One way altcourse is a bit different to armley is theres not so much drugs at least not as obvious. Some lads take diazepams or valiums mainly the ones that were using heroin before they come inside George I suppose you'd know all about that being a copper. I don't bother with that its not the same as a drink is it. I had diazepams when I first come in and I don't like the memory of that Ive seen the lads on them theyre good for nothing. Drink makes you lively it's a laugh isn't it. Its not perfect I admit I drank too much sometimes lose my memory. Used to be funny that folk telling us what Id done but you do lose little bits of your life George. Thing with getting older George is each time you get that drunk its like you lose a bit of what you remembered from before too not just the bit when you were drunk but a piece of before. Its like your brain gets a bit soggy George wet and woolly.

After I sent that one to the mirror I got a bit jumpy George. I shouldn't have bothered because no one took the blindest bit of notice did they. You lot just went on doing what you do but not catching anyone. I went on signing on and spending my social security on drink. You could drink for a week on one giro cheque in them days George not like now. I drank a lot then George. Did do some work on sites. Every now and then someone would have something Come round pick up a bunch of lads in a van go and do a job somewhere in Penshaw or Seaham sometimes Cleadon posh that like. But there wasn't much of that George just every now and then.

Still went to the library still nicked in at the pictures. Played darts at the Robin went to the Shipwrights. Every now and then one of the lads from school come into some spond and we had a beano went for a drink in Barnes park at the bandstand. Used to go Seaburn hall or the Boilermakers to see bands whenever we had a few quid spare tried the punk bands at the mecca not really my scene George the jam maybe sham 69 not really sure I was quite pissed. Jethro Tull was more my kind of thing thin lizzy motorhead.

I think that one was a cold winter its difficult to remember that though isn't it George which winters were cold which summers were hot. They were all shit probably. Rain. The things that never went away was the smell of hops the sound of seagulls the sounds like explosions from the yards. Only the seagulls left out of that lot now George, They must be feeling nervous.

Your faithful friend

Jack the ripper

PE8133 HMP Altcourse, Fazakerley, 2nd April 2007

Dear George,

I've been here a few months now. I suppose Busters the
one I speak to most even though you cant get too friendly
inside no point people get moved around the system all the
time, One day theyre here next day they're gone.

Now George I know you know what goes on in prison I
think its disgusting personally and I don't think youd approve
either I'm not much of a one for puffs and you cant be a part-
time queer if you ask me but some lads in prison say they are
They say theyre just queer while theyre inside. Its mainly the
lads that are here longest. I guess its either that or wanking if
youre bothered. So theres this one lad called Geoff and hes
queer for Dobbo. Dobbo was a gangster on the outside local
lad did all sorts of drug smuggling into Liverpool hes a big
cheese in here George.

This afternoon Geoff comes into busters cell looking sick
as a dog says he can't think what else to do hes tried everything can Buster help him. Says hell give Buster twenty
phonecards Offers to suck him off Buster says don't worry
about that son the phonecardsll do fine whats the problem.

Our Geoffs been writing letters to dobbos bird on the sly
and they've been sending each other photographs not family
friendly george if you get my drift. Dobbos birds a bit of a
slapper "no offence" she started writing to geoff after seeing

him at visiting this once and geoff got a kick out of going behind dobbos back with his own missus.

So Busters just shaking his head thinking what a buggers muddle and trying to work out how to let the lad down but Geoff carries on with his story. So Dobbos bird Hayley has sent geoff this snap of her that doesn't leave much to the imagination and geoffs having a perv over it when in walks dobbo with Clarky his pet screw. Geoffs panicking but he puts the photo face down on his cot so theres only the writing on the back says Im keeping hot for you lover boy or something on the back signed H xx. Dobbo doesn't notice hes going on about someone that's doing his head in but Clarkys spotted straightaway that geoffs spooked. While dobbos talking to geoff clarky slides the photo into his pocket. Dobbo lets off his steam and clarky and dobbo bugger off again. After that geoff knows hes in deep trouble and all the next week he's panicking about what dobbos going to do to him.

Nothing happens but clarky keeps giving him a nudge and wink winding him up. Geoffs not daft He knows clarkys got one over on him as long as hes got the photo of Hayley Hes going on and on about it how its been purloined. He knows hes got to get it back. So Buster says whats this got to do with me. Geoff says well Ive tried to get it back. Geoffs owed favours off a lot of people being Dobbos friend and he calls some of these favours in off lads on the cleaning rota who go into the guards quarters all the time. Between them they've been through the whole place given it the once over the twice over checked everywhere. They've checked the bookshelves in the books everywhere. Geoff must have some big favours because this one lads even managed to have a squizz in Clarkys locker if hed got caught doing that Lord alone knows what would of happened to him six months in segregation probably. Geoffs at his wits end and hes come to buster cause Busters liaison for the wing and because everyone knows hes the cleverest bastard anyway.

Buster says hell give it a whirl but dont hold out much hope. Hes got to go into the guards room this evening to do some admin with Clarky about a complaint one of the lads has made.

Ill tell you how that turns out George its our own little thriller.

Keeping hot for you George

Saucy Jack

PE8133 HMP Altcourse, Fazakerley, 5th April 2007

Dear George,

Well you would not believe it but busters geoffs hero Says hes practically having to fight him off hes that happy. yes george Buster got the photo back for geoff.

When he was in the guards room with clarky doing the admin two nights ago buster mentioned that geoff was acting strange seemed really down and he was worried about him. This is part of busters job wing liaison has to keep an eye out for lads with depression and at risk. Buster says clarky laughed it off said something like just a lovers tiff probably itll blow over but as soon as buster had mentioned geoffs name clarkys eyes had flicked over to this picture on the shelf in the guards room above the bin. On the shelf theres a framed porno picture and immediately buster knows hes found Hayley. Not that youd be able to tell from the picture says buster unless you were her gyneycologist. He says nowt just finishes business and goes back to his cell.

Next day buster asks for the lend of a porno off Tom before Tom knows whats up he finds a picture and cuts it out Tom was screaming blue murder Whats wrong with you I loved that picture Buster says not to worry hell get him a new porno. After bangup he goes to have a word with geoff and that evening hes back in the guards room to finish up the admin with clarky with his porno picture tucked in his back pocket.

middle of the meeting theres a knock at guards room door and its this lad Edgar Allen telling clarky someones going off their nut on the twos clarky says give us five minutes buster and hes away to sort it out. Buster goes to the photo of Hayley takes it out the frame and puts the one hes cut out of the porno mag in its place. Buster says you wouldn't know the difference so just to make sure hes written don't you like me better big boy on the back. He puts it back above the bin and when clarky comes back in saying whole thing was a lot of fuss over nothing he doesnt bat an eyelid they finish there meeting and that's that

So Busters geoffs hero now and hes got more phonecards than he knows what to do with Toms got a brand new porno and its chocolate biscuits all round. Buster says its all daft because he doesn't think even dobbo would have recognized Hayley from this picture but geoffs chuffed hes in the clear. Clarky looks a bit confused but that's clarky and he doesn't wink at geoff anymore in fact geoff winks at him.

Its too good to be true that isn't it George. I'm keeping a poe-face.

Jolly Jack Tar

PE8133 HMP Altcourse, Fazakerley, 14th April 2007

Dear George,

I have started a writing course. I don't expect you will think that is strange since you know my writing as well as anyone George. We get extra credits for doing any courses and I am interested in improving my writing even though I am functionally literate as judge jones said some people who have read my best writing think it is not very good particularly the grammar. So I will work hard to improve.

The lad who takes the writing is called Martyn. He is a decent sort calls everyone by their first name has a laugh with all the lads. The first lesson was just chatting about the course and what we like to read. It was surprising what some of the lads liked George there's this big Scottish lad called Kenneth he looks like a nutter George but he says he likes to read poetry. Tom the mong likes drug books he said like Irvine welsh everyone knows that trainspotting and most lads nodded. There was a lot that agreed on all the SAS books bravo 2 zero and that kind of thing so no surprise there really. This one lad gimpo they call him from Manchester said he was into crime but Id never heard of any of the writers he was talking about Gordon burnside or someone American too. I said I liked crime too but mostly true crime. Martyn said that it was important to have different opinions we would all learn if we listened to each other.

Of course there were some lads in the group who didn't even know what they were there for. This is a gaol George and not everyone is very bright. This one lad called Barry thought he was going to learn to do that fancy handwriting. That was a laugh we all had a chuckle at that. Martyn has said first of all not to worry about spelling and grammar well that is a relief for me as you might of guessed but it is even better for some of the other lads who can barely hold a pen George.

Martyn says we will be building towards writing from our experiences. We will start off with simple exercises and they will get more complicated. The first one he has set us is to describe something anything that is near to us in the prison or in our cells. he says to try to say everything we can about it to think about it every way.

He says next week we will start properly with descriptions and we will have homework. Everyone moaned when he said that it was just like being at school George. I will show you my first exercise when I have finished it.

I think I have run out of things to say to you George about my life outside my life before. I think that is it I should probably stop writing now. If there is anything else you would like to know you should just ask.

Alright George I will stop pulling your leg. There is certainly one story you and your friends would like to know that is the story of your favourite song that Andrew Gold one.

Once upon a time I decided to make a tape because I thought it would be a laugh. I knew you would be interested to hear more from me. I could imagine you sitting there listening to me with your red face and I thought that would be a hoot. I thought about phoning but I didn't want to risk that didn't want a trace on the call but I did want to get more personal. All along George I just wanted to be friends too

I suppose we are friends know aren't we Penfriends at any rate.

I must have walked into town the usual way through the crem through the yids burial ground past the general hospital. Can't remember George but this is the way I always went climbed over the wall into the crem liked looking at all the gravestones amount of times I was chased by some gadgey in a big black overcoat that was part of the fun. I can even remember the names George. Roderick Stanley. Jacqueline Spears. Harold Gilroy. Susan Curry. Victor Robson. Always daffodils in my memory. Names changed in the jews burial ground. Seth Jacobson. Henry Lando.

I went to Boots. Boots was always the best place to buy tapes cheaper than woollies they had them upstairs next to the records near the homebrew. I tried making homebrew once George it was howfing tasted like puke I'd rather have the puke after thanks very much. I'd drink it now mind you I'd drink anything now.

I bought a c60 I didn't have that much to say George. A nice short message just for you. I'd written it down like I wrote the letters it was about the same length. I know Gavin Weale would of loved to have seen that piece of paper and mr bromley-hughes QC they would have loved it. what I wrote is very valuable to the right people.

I had written down the words just like in a letter. I suppose I would have come back on the bus I sometimes walked back from town but more often than not I took the number 20 up hylton road.

I didn't have to wait for my mam to go out cause she wasn't there when I got back she was at work. I'd decided on the little song just for you a little bit of country eh George a bit of a giggle that. I bought a copy especially can you believe that.

20p at durham book centre for the cassette. Or maybe Id bought that before I can't remember.

I needed to do the first bit when my mam was out. I practiced reading the letter George. Read it five times or more. I'm Jack. I see you are still having no luck catching me. I'm Jack. I see you are still having no luck catching me Etc Etc. I used the timer on my watch used to have one of them digital watches all the rage back then. 4 minutes it took to read if I went good and slow and I was taught at school to read slow out loud so people could understand.

Stanley had a twin deck radio cassette recorder in his room. He was dead proud of it used to tape the radio and make copies of his best songs. I went in stanley's room and put the Andrew Gold tape in one side and the blank tape in the other side. I pressed record and pause then I started the Andrew Gold tape and took the blank tape off pause. The song started playing and the tape started recording. I let it play all the way through then I stopped it. It lasted for 4 minutes and 23 seconds.

I took both tapes out and I went back to my own room. I had a Ferguson in my room and a little microphone I'd got at Currys. I put the blank tape in and I plugged the microphone into the jack. I rewound the tape. I put my letter on the bed and I pressed record and pause. I got ready with the microphone and with the timer on my watch and when I was ready I started recording and then I started reading. I made sure I took good breaths and I went nice and slow. I had to pause the tape a couple of times First time I needed a rest Second time I thought I heard a noise. Third time I nearly lost my place. I read it all nice and easy and then I pressed stop I rewound the whole tape and listened back to it.

It sounded pretty good George if I say so myself. It

sounded like the ripper would sound if he was from Sunderland. I had a little giggle at the song at the end, shall we sing the words together?

Thank you for being a friend
You're the best friend a man could have
You're as honest as the day is long
A friend that's true, a bond that's strong
I know that we will always be
Friends together, you and me
When we have a get-together
All your pals at a jamboree
I'll bring your present inscribed from me
The message to you, personally,
Thank you for being a friend
Thank you for being a friend
Thank you for being a friend
Thank you for being a friend

there was a bit of a gap but that was okay. I hope you did like it. I got all excited then that I'd done it I got a bit excited and bit worried. I thought that I would have to clean the tape because tapes aren't like letters I thought I'd better take the label off. I peeled the label away but not all of it would come off so I went downstairs to the kitchen and got a knife out the drawer and used that to scrape off the rest. Then I got a bit worked up about cleaning the tape George. I thought I'd better clean it inside just in case. I found a small Phillips head screwdriver in the drawer and started trying to open the cassette to clean inside and then I thought I was being stupid so I stopped. There was nothing inside the tape was there George. I might of broken it and undone all my hard work. The reports said there was custard powder on the tape Ive no idea how that got there.

I found a stamp from my mam's purse in the living room and I found an envelope. I wrote out the address from the newspapers. I took care not to leave any fingerprints then gloves were very useful. I walked round to ford road and popped it in the post box and then I went to the pub The Jackdaw I think.

Bit of a day that was eh George.

Your pal

Jack the Giantkiller

WRITING EXERCISE 1
DESCRIPTION
By John Samuel Humble

My cell at Leeds gaol looked like this. There was a netty in the corner with a curtain round it that we made from odds and sods scavenged from the laundry and stitched together by deafie. There was a metal sink on the wall next to the bog. There were four walls with some pictures on them cut out of magazines SAFC team photo Deafie's lass some page three stunner. In one wall was the iron door with a sliding slot it can only be slid from the outside. There was a metal bunk bed with two bunks with mattresses pillows and grey prison covers. Deafie has the top bunk because hes younger than me I thought this was a kind gesture but I've been farted on so much I'm not so certain. There is not much else to say about this cell except for one bit on the underneath of deafie's mattress. I looked at this bit for so long that it is like a floater in front of my eyes or inside my eyeball, It is a small bit of frayed stuff around one of the buttons like they have on most mattresses. Why they have buttons on mattresses I don't know perhaps you do. It pokes between the wire mesh of the bottom of the bunk. This bit of frayed stuff has lots of colours in it mostly grey but also some brown yellow red and blue. Its like the guts of the mattress leaking out. I picked at it one time and more came out in a big string so I never picked at it again but I could have pulled all the insides of Deafies mattress out onto the floor and it would have been neater but Im not that bothered about it being neat. I would bet my bottom dollar that that bit of stuff is still hanging out the bottom of deafie's mattress but I don't know who'll be underneath it now or if theyve even noticed.

John,

This is a really good start. You've embraced the exercise and applied yourself to describing something in detail. I was really struck by the fact that you chose to do something from memory. That's really good practice for writing. I have to say it has a very distinct voice, it is recognisably yours.

You should try to avoid repetition and words such as 'stuff' or 'some' that do little descriptive work. Every word has to pull its weight; a piece of writing is a bit like a football team, in this sense: you can carry some players who are tired or not very talented but the fewer there are, the better the team will be.

To that end, I'd like to see you working towards using a larger vocabulary. I've asked Philip in the library to make dictionaries and thesauruses available to all the students in this class so please try to get hold of these from him. They are invaluable aids in your writing practice.

But as I say, this is a really good first piece. Well done. I look forward to reading your next one.

Martyn

TRANSCRIPT OF GEORGE OLDFIELD'S STATEMENT TO THE PRESS AT POLICE ACADEMY, WAKEFIELD, 26th June 1979

Well, we already know quite a lot about him. The big thing from the tape and the interesting thing as far as we're concerned is that it narrows down our field of inquiry. We know now that we are definitely looking for a man who originated in the North East and we've been able to localise it down to the Sunderland area of the North East.

I am convinced this is the man who murdered eleven women.

Handwriting experts are sure that the man who addressed the envelope which contained the cassette was the same person who wrote the previous letters.

In those previous letters, there was information about the murders which could only really be known by the killer. He seems to see it as some sort of duel and I am prepared to duel. There can only be one winner in the end.

I am satisfied that the tape and the three letters are from the same man and it is my belief he is the man we are seeking. There is no doubt he was born in Sunderland or the Sunderland area.

PE8133 HMP Altcourse, Fazakerley, 21st October 2007

Dear George,

It all came home in one go. Not difficult to remember the day it changed my life. Tuesday 26th June the headline on the echo Ripper is a Wear Man. That lunchtime on all the news bulletins there you were playing my tape. Id picked a fight with you George was the way you saw it a duel. You said there can only be one winner. Im sad to say George that you were wrong there wasn't a winner.

I wasn't expecting it George it had been nearly two weeks since Id posted it and not a squeak. All of a sudden it was on all the news you sat there looking redfaced You Dick Holland and some other copper. You looked sad George not angry. The other two looked angry deadly serious. It was a shock George. I kept telling myself it sounded strangled. I hadnt heard it since Id made it I never played it back did I. My mam saw it on the news that night if she recognised my voice she didn't let on. I was jumpy George started mumbling swallowing up my words when anyone spoke to us. It kept jumping out on us my voice. Turn on the radio there it was on the news. Days and days of it. Anyone could've told it was me. I didn't go out the first few days I was waiting for the heat to die down. Had to go out a bit or my mam would've got suspicious but just went and kicked around in the crem.

They had the phone line up for the weekend. Call

Sunderland 43146. Grass your mates. I kept thinking who would grass on us. Could be anyone Geoff Robin maybe even Cora. Like a cat on a hot tin roof. Like that feller in that film. My voice everywhere. I dialled the number and listened to the recording George did me duty as a good citizen. It didn't even sound like me all that crackle on the line it was difficult to tell who it sounded like but it sounded like someone else. it sounded bit like him to be honest. I wasn't sure it was me but I knew it was I did it didn't I no one else. My doing and a phone number to call just to hear my voice. I wondered if you lot could tell who'd phoned up if you kept a record of all the numbers that phoned and listened. Can they do that I bet they can. stanley was telling us about all the bugging they do in northern Ireland all the intelligence they're always listening in to the IRA so if they can do that they might have this number. But then why would they be bothered about whose phoning I mean its not like its a trap is it. They want everyone to listen don't they thats why they've set up the line like this so everyone can listen to my voice.

I thought to myself George I don't think Im going do much talking just now in case anyone hears us.

That Friday Doris Stokes was on the telly. Me mam wanted to watch it so I went out. Bumped into Gary Walker in The Wharfe. Everyone was talking about it everyone saying it sounded like so and so that sound s like you marrah youre the ripper no youre the ripper. Everyone was the ripper. You had to laugh George. Some lads took it dead serious If I find the ripper before the police Ill have his fucking guts for garters. Cant believe hes from sunderland. Whys he killing prozzies down there theres loads at the Bridge Hotel. but for most lads it was a big joke a pisstake. Lads had phoned up the lines said

I know who it is its Pop Robson he's a ripper. I felt a bit better hearing that.

Geoff said he'd been in The Shipwrights straight after knock-off and there was this gadgey from Yorkshire with a tape recorder asking people to speak into his microphone. Said he was going all up the river stopping off in pubs and recording voices. Looking for a match to the tape said Geoff a expert.

No one knew what to make of that George. It was my voice what he was looking for he wasn't going to find it in The Shipwrights.

Stayed in bed all the saturday. When I got up me mam made us listen to the radio. She said this is important this he's been inside cherry knowle. I didn't say nowt because me mam took all that stuff deadly serious but it give me fits listening to it it really did. This Doris Stokes was being interviewed about her TV programme when she'd tried to make contact with the killer and she said when she heard the recording she knew it was rehearsed. I was glad she'd noticed the work that had gone in to be honest George. she said she thought I was trying to disguise my voice and she was beginning to get things a bit wrong then wasn't she. Then she said I thought I'm hearing Gateshead I heard a lady crying from the other side very emotional and this lady she said something about a mental hospital and I heard ch and then it sounded like cherry and I said that's ridiculous I suppose and I thought that is ridiculous pet I wonder how that happened. I don't think you could of found out about cherry knowle by reading books or papers or talking to people or anything it must be important in some way she said and then I took on the personality of the man and I became very agitated and my left eye started twitching and I knew by then this person is a split personality and then the interviewer said a dr Jekyll and mr hyde sort of person and she said yes and I think I've got a scar. Honestly George I was creased up trying not to let on to me mam how funny this was I wanted to say it sounds like our jerry because jerry's got a big scar down his face from an accident at Austin and pickersgill but I didn't. It sounded like someone out of a hammer horror film I wanted to say and he wears a cape mam and he's got a hunchback. But I kept schtum and several other things came through I can usually tell ages by voice she said he's about thirty one or thirty two and I thought only ten year out and she said another voice came through and it was very confused and I thought that's the first thing you've got right petal. honestly this was about the funniest thing and me mam taking it all seriously like it was gospel truth George. She said I was about the same height as her husband and that she'd told us to hand meself in because you were going to catch us. Maybe she did have something after all George only thirty year out on that one. But honestly what I was thinking is you can't bullshit a bullshitter.

That weekend there was extracts from my letter in the papers. Lord I was glad I had done my handwriting different slanted it to the side George. I didn't expect anyone to recognise it really not that many people see your handwriting maybe my mam. Then that Sunday walking down hylton road I saw Mr Campbell my old English teacher and I crossed the road to not say hello. That had me worried that did but then again I suppose he sees that much crap writing.

George it got worse and worse around then. The next week plainclothes squads were all over Castletown playing my voice in the pubs The Mickey Mouse playing it in the clubs No one noticed or if they did they said nowt to me or the police. Made me wonder if anyone ever listened to me. I kept a lid on it.

There was no need my voice was doing all the talking for us It didn't need me anymore.

Thing is George there was a time that summer everyone was listening to my voice I was listening to my voice you couldn't not listen to my voice it was playing everywhere wasn't it. It was playing out the top of the police caravan they had parked on Castle View not much point having a caravan and not moving it about but youve never been the brightest tools in the box have you george. Ivy Kennedy come round ours one teatime said shed been asked by a TV reporter if shed heard the tape and she said only every fucking hour pet coming out that caravan. It was playing at the Odeon I was hiding under the seats before The Hills Have Eyes and there was my voice playing out the speakers.

It was playing out of tape recorders carried by the tecs that were going around town two by two. Going everywhere knocking on every door playing my voice. Hylton Castle Red House, Downhill Town End Farm. Wrong side of water like but all the same. Coppers with clipboards pens forms tape recorders test tubes. Like fat scientists with bad breath and BO.

I was sat in the Robins with Steve Harper and this pair of coppers come in with a little Ferguson tape recorder and played it to everyone in the bar. Everyone was listening like theyd not heard it before everyone wanted to impress the bizzies seem like they were helping. The one with the tape recorder says you've probably heard this voice a lot the past few days but we want you all to think very hard because we're certain that someone knows who it is and some feller at the bar says Its the ripper isn't it. And the bizzy has a chuckle well we think so just listen again for us will you and he presses down the rewind till the tape hits the tracks and presses down the play button on the tape recorder and the voice comes out again It was' nt difficult for me to act along like I dint know who it was because it didnt sound like me. It sounded lower pitched and weedy and lispy it sounded nothing like me but I looked like I was listening carefully and when it got to the song at the end I had to try hard not to chuckle that Andrew gold song I recorded for you George. someone sat at the bar a feller with work boots on said he's got shit taste in music hasn't he and everyone laughed at that like it released the tension and then someone says that sounds like a durham accent that does. And someone else says don't be daft that's sunderland that is thats castletown. the first feller says thats what everyone thinks because that's what theyve told us but that sounds like Durham that does crook or somewhere up the river. nah marrah that's never durham pipes up lad. That sounds like pitmatic that does pitmatic someone laughs that's nowt like pitmatic. pitmatic's not an accent growls an old gadgey who's sat at table in the corner. there's as many different types of pitmatic as there are pits There 's no pitmatic in that he says. where do you think its from Harold asks the lad with the boots. Hes from Sunderland that's for sure close round here and hes young you can tell that. The tec pipes up and says the experts havent given any indication of age so dont rule anything out. You saying Doris stoke's not an expert asks one lad and everyone laughs again. Aye it's prob-ably Harold says the lad at the bar and a couple of the others laugh at him Harold's been killing prozzies for years man Harold just looks at him and grunts. no hard feelings man Harold says the lad I was only pulling your leg. How jammer give Harold a drink or he'll gan off in a huff probably do me in too sorry Harold man I was just joking but harold's not finished and he says if you lot knew any pitmatic you would'nt talk such clarts. Everyones pissing themselves and Harold gets angry you've no idea about you're own heritage. how many of you had fathers that worked in pits how many had uncles. Aye says a lad but nay one's working now are they. And everyone laughs again the bizzie's not in the picture he tries to get control back. seriously lads please have a good think. And there's lots of muttering and Charlie harper says to me you got any idea john and I say sounds a bit like davver And Charlie says nah I thought it sounded a bit like your stanley. So I say I don't think thats stanleys kind of game that he gets enough lasses without having to do them in and Charlie says you're not wrong there.

I tried to change the way I spoke George pretended I had a cold spoke through my nose. one night in the jackdaw dave said you're sounding a bit funny john lad you're not sounding yourself. if I said too much someone was going to put two and two together but they didn't did they because they didn't notice I wasn't talking cause they never listened to us in the first place anyway.

It was everyone george everyone. The Jamesons lived next door to us in Halsted Square. Cath was the mam Ernie was the dad They had two bairns called Sid and Samantha. They were always in the garden Ernie wasn't that much older than me and stanley early thirties or something but because he was a dad he seemed that much older. He worked as foreman at a tyre depot in the Team Valley and he had a car He thought he was something special. Ernie did 'nt trust me George. He thought I was a bad lot because I was on the dole and because I had a record. He was probably right but he didn't know did he George and that used to get right up my nose He kept telling us to get out and get a job. He couldn't keep his neb out. I remember seeing Ernie in the front yard of his house when I come back from town one day that summer and he called us over. John lad How John lad.

He said have the coppers had you in yet. I said what do you mean. He said For the ripper. I said nah and Ernie said well thats rich that is. They've had me in and I'm a family man They should've had you. He looked at us suspicious like it was my fault they'd had him in. I said What did they ask you. Where I worked If I went to Yorkshire. Then they give us a sheet with all these samples on it from the letters and that and had us copy it out see if my handwriting matched the letters.

George my heart nearly jumped out my mouth. I wanted to puke. I'd been keeping quiet Id been keeping my head low and now You lot were next door. Ernie carried on regardless. He said they're coming round door-to-door now for the handwriting and saliva. Theyll catch up with you sooner or later, When he said that George I thought I was done for. I thought he knew I did n't want to look at his face but I had to and when I looked I knew I was alright. He had this like jealous look in his eyes He was only bothered because they'd not had me in and they'd had him. He didn't know.

But after that George I couldn't stay in unless there was no one else in. If my mam was home I had to go out If your lot came round when my mam was in she'd call us down to do the writing. If I was in on my own I could ignore the bell and stay hid in my room. If anyone else was in Cora or anyone I'd not be able to do that Not much choice then George but to stay down the pub.

Next day at the shipwrights Alan howe had one of these sheets. I said give us a look at that alan. Not much like my words George all neatly typed out. Some bits from me Sorry I havn't written. Too bloody hot.

I wonder George did you choose which words to use for

that. It was an odd feeling seeing them there in type my words some of them some them his words some of them Jacks some of them yours. I wonder what would of happened if they had asked me to write them out Would I have been able to write different enough. I don' t know George and Im glad I never had to find out. But it was very strange those words were n't mine anymore they were on that sheet all typed out. Alan Howe wanted to keep the sheet He said he had his suspicions and there was this lad he wanted to check out. That gave me a giggle that did. But folk were dead suspicious of each other it was only me not suspicious.

The other thing was everyone was hopping mad at what was in the papers all this flat caps and whippets crap. It was bad enough they were calling me a Geordie but then they were coming into pubs these TV reporters from the south of England and asking everyone what they did. could we film your pigeon loft. Whats it like down the pits. Is the community pulling together. The community was grassing on anyone weird anyone fat anyone dirty just like every community would. I wasn't much interested in getting found out then George. Just keep a lid on it that was the best plan.

Not much to tell you about whats going on in here. Buster has give us a loan of one of his phones George. thats another thing that is different in here is more mobile phones. Lots of the lads have them they don't have the nets here George they get smuggled in chucked over the walls. Buster has two phones three different sim cards that go in them. the cards make them work like the cards for watching the football on sky. Lads at home used to have cards ripped off from Sweden that let you watch as much football as you like for nowt they show all the games over there Alan howe had one. These cards are for phones.

I've no one to call George no one to text. Its not much use to me.

More tomorrow George more everyday

Jack the Ripper

Dictate the following text to the subject and have them copy it out on the pro-forma provided:

Dear James,

Tell Auntie Elsie I will be home soon. I have already written to Mum and told her of my travel plans. I am sorry that I haven't written sooner. Thank you for that photo.

I am looking forward to being up North again. Too bloody hot down here.

Yours sincerely

George

PE8133 HMP Altcourse, Fazakerley, 13th November 2007

Dear George,

I have a good story that I thought you would appreciate it gives me the fits anyway. I have had my first piece of paid work in gaol. It was not much one day stuffing xmas crackers. Xmas is a sad time in here lads all missing theyre families so this was not like normal where lads would be queing up for the job to get some extra spon. The job is like this Theres a box of jokes a box of folded hats and some boxes of little plastic gifts. Theres hopping frogs that you make jump theres little keyrings theres plastic snowmen theres whistles and theres the little black moustaches that clip on your nose. Then theres the half crackers. The lads have to put one of each thing in the crackers and put them together. Theres a guard watching closely so no one nicks all the snaps from in the middle and makes a bomb. Thats a laugh that right George. When theyve got all the crackers together they put them in boxes its meant to be a good old mix up so everyone gets a bit of everything. Well of course the lads are trying out all the toys for a crack theres frogs pinging everywhere This one lad tries on the moustache and does a Hitler impression with nazi salutes and achtung achtung ve hav vays of making you talk all that. All the rest of us were falling about wetting ourselves.

One of the lads at that bench has a brainwave and he tells his pals. This lot don't mix up the crackers after that all their crackers have hitler moustaches every single one. We were all pissing ourselves too when we imagined that works xmas party with 24 hitlers care of HMP altcourse.

But I must not forget what were really writing about here. You need everything don't you George. Facts and that. Not how i pass my time in prison.

It was a long summer that George. Not much weather which suited me I was staying indoors. Your pals in Sunderland were working hard for their wages Hard slog on the wrong side of the water mainly. Caravan moved taking my voice with it. I kept quiet but your lot kept looking. Fred Horner told us they had a squad in the sorting depot checking every single letter. I wasn't writing much then George only writing I did was signing on. Posters went up everywhere with my handwriting I was just hoping they wouldn't go up in the dole office. I kept an eye on the papers it was hard to read. Sickening. Disgusting. Disgraceful. I knew how people felt by reading the papers George.

There was lots in the echo mainly about what you lot were up to I suppose they didn't have a lot to report on me. I did have a laugh though George when they were writing about other lads whod phoned in pretending to be me or lads with mackem accents nicked in yorkshire.

Made a change from stories about Sunderlands centenary year. Coppers were all over the games and Im not surprised. I saw match of the day and you could hear the chants. Theres only one Yorkshire ripper. 12 nil to the ripper. Youll never catch the ripper. Jimmy Hill and Bob Wilson acted like they were deaf but we all heard.

That time was difficult for me George. This one time we've been sat in The Bridge and Pat Spencer's come in and he's said lads fancy coming to the game and Stanley says you're not saying you've got tickets and Pat says aye I was in town in The Coach and this hairy comes in he's from the polytechnic and he recognises us from the Locarno and he comes and sits next to us and says he's looking for some tack do I know anyone and I says I've got some tack back home and he says is it any good is it like red leb or something like that red leb for fucks sake where does he think he is fucking Amsterdam and I says look marrah its from Hartlepool and its proper gear it'll get you and your student mates stoned off your head and this lad says alright then I'll have some of that that sounds good. Stanley says to Pat you've not got any tack and Pat says aye well this lad doesn't know that does he so I says I'll be back in twenty minutes you get yourself a pint and I goes out down Fawcett Street and Im thinking what can I get that looks like tack and I find this piece of dried shit on the ground Im' serious it's dried shit it's like hard and black and I'm not joking it's perfect. Stanley says you fucking better be joking and Pat laughs and says I'm not fucking joking and then I bump into me auntie Eileen and she's coming back from the shops and she's got some cling film in her bag and Im thinking this is too good to be true this and I get a bit of cling film off auntie Eileen and she thinks am tapped she's thinking I've gone off me rocker but she's soft as clarts me auntie Eileen so she gives us some anyway so I wrap this little bit of shit in the clingfilm and go back down The Coach and this lad's there and I slide it under the table to him and says that's fifteen quid and he says that's pretty good for a quarter and I says I've got fucking loads more where that came from and he's about to open up the cling film and give it a sniff or something and I says not in here son I fucking drink in here and he says it better be good and I says listen son if you and your mates don't get high off that my name's not Stanley Humble. And

Stanley looks at Pat and says you never said that you fucking charver and Pat says of course I did I don't want that coming back to haunt us do I and I just laugh he's a pisstaker our Pat. anyway says Pat I thought I'd make it up to you for using your name in vane so I've spent the money on tickets for the match and what do you know Johnny lad I've bought one for you too and I says mint cheers for that Pat and he says nay bother so we have another couple of pints and set off to roker and we're all full of it man on Lorimers and that bit wobbly and having a laugh about Pat how he could sell shit for a living and Pat likes the sound of that and what'll it be like when the lad from the poly burns that shit and it's fucking class that and we cross the Wear Bridge and it looks beautiful out there there's the sound of seagulls and the air is all salt and hops from the brewery its Sunderland through and through and there's lads singing all the songs on the way to the game everyone's walking across the bridge cause it's matchday everyone in town's ganning to the game everyone who's got enough for a ticket at any rate and we walk down and we go in the stands at Fulwell end and its crowded but the atmosphere's something special and everyone's singing and we're joining in all the songs and then there's a new one and I don't recognise it and I don't even hear the words at first it takes us a few seconds to tune in and then I hear it and I cannt stop my head from spinning cause they're all singing I know jack the ripper jack the ripper knows me the whole of roker park and my head's spinning cause it's everyone in town at the game. And they're all singing this taking the piss and Pat's pissing himself and Stanley's pissing himself and they're all joining in singing. I know jack the ripper jack the ripper knows me. and it's fucking hilarious and Stanley nudges us but Im not really there George I'm like a foot above my own head and watching from on high as I start singing I know jack the ripper jack the ripper knows me and I don't know if I'm gonna pass out I know jack the ripper jack the ripper knows me and the sound fades back like a wave some people still singing some stopped and some getting quieter but Im still singing I know jack the ripper jack the ripper knows me and Stanley looks at us and says you can stop now John.

ROKER GROUND STAFF

Fred Harley has been a Sunderland fan since he was six years old – and he's now 44. For the last eight years he has worked at Roker Park and as Stadium Manager he has supervised the spending of many thousands of pounds to make the stadium what it is today.

He has strong views on football fans and on what he wants to see at the ground in the coming years. He talked frankly to ROKER REVIEW last week and is convinced that if people would only stop and think when they are inside Roker Park everybody would enjoy their football much more.

"Let me make it quite clear from the start that when we talk about football hooliganism and violence we are talking about a small minority of fans – and Sunderland's record in this respect is not a bad one," he begins.

"But it could be better – and I won't be satisfied until it is better. I am totally convinced that obscene chanting, never mind direct violence, caused thousands of would-be fans to stay away from Roker Park and other grounds.

"It amazes me that some people can go to a football ground and chant obscenities for minutes on end. They wouldn't do it in their home, in a theatre or cinema, so why think of doing it at Roker Park?

"It sickens me that decent folk have to be subjected to this obscene chanting – and I know that many have given up coming to football matches for this reason alone.

"It feels as if there is something of a cloud over the town at the moment and this behaviour does our sense of self no good at all."

ANOTHER CHANCE TO WIN! £5

Each home programme will feature a lucky face and the winner will win a crisp £5 note. Providing he can produce this programme to, Timothy Irwin, Secretary's Office, Roker Park.

The Man Next to You May Have Killed 12 Women

He may be sitting or standing next to you in your pub, club or canteen. Or in a queue. Or on a bus. He may be working at the next machine, desk or table. But he is in fact a vicious, deranged maniac, whose method of murder and mutilation is so sick that it has turned the stomachs of even the most hardened of police officers. Here's how you can help. Look closely at the handwriting. It's the writing of a sadistic killer. And if you think you recognise it from a note, letter, envelope, signature, cheque, anything, report it to your local police. Listen to the killer's voice. By phoning Sunderland 43146 you can hear probably the most important clue to the killer's identity. His voice. It won't be a pleasant experience but it could lead to the end of these brutal murders. If you think you recognise the voice, tell the police.

PE8133 HMP Altcourse, Fazakerley, 29th December 2007

Dear George.

It was unstoppable my voice and I should know I tried to stop it. I phoned twice George to tell them it was a hoax. They played the tapes back to me when I told them that this summer. I said fat lot of good that did. we didn't believe you they said and I told them that was pretty obvious. It was a Wednesday night and I'd been down the star and I'd been drinking on me own because I was avoiding micky and jammer all they were ever taking about was jack this and jack that and I couldn't bear it anymore. Then the lad behind the bar said you heard the latest on jack and I lost it I couldn't get away from it could I, I just lost it and said everyone's just going on and on about jack this and jack that I said its probably just some kid having a laugh and the lad behind the bar said nah no way marrah its real that is have you not heard it its definitely him. I just turned on me heels and marched straight to the phone box I couldn't believe it was still going on. It was getting worsen that. Everyone believed it everyone in town. I went into the phone box and I looked up the number for gill bridge and I phoned it. I wanted to tell you George. I got through first time and I just blurted it out then i hung up. I thought they might be tracing the call like on the telly. I thought they might come and get us. I went back in the star and had another pint. The lad behind the bar asked if I was alright. Aye I said I'm fine this jack stuff its getting us down. People say I sound like him. The lad says aye well you do a bit.

No hanging up now George

Day of the Jackal

Mount: Repeat that, I can't hear you, it's a bad line.

Caller: Tell him it's a fake.

Mount: What's a fake?

Caller: The tape recording.

Mount: What one is this?

Caller: The one that he's just received. The Ripper tape recording.

Mount: Aha. How do you know that?

Caller: Just tell him.

Mount: Just tell him?

Caller: The one in June.

Mount: Pardon?

Caller: The one in June.

Mount: I'm sorry it's a bad—

Caller: . . . Sorry

Mount: It's a bad line; you're going to have to repeat it.

(Caller hangs up)

PE8133 HMP Altcourse, Fazakerley, 2nd January 2008

Dear George,

I wonder what you would be reading now if you were alive. Not the Guardian probably because they are mean bastards aren't they George. I am reading all sorts George not since I was in school have I been reading this much. The library here is very good it's a nice place to go.

In my writing class I was worried about my grammar George. It is not very good as you know especially not my punctuation. I told the lad Martyn and he told me not to worry. He said it was more important that I was able to find the right voice. He said that what he'd read of mine showed I had an authentic voice. I don't think he knows what I'm in for George do you? I am worried about my punctuation. It's hard not to be people pay a lot of attention to my full stops and commas George. I wanted to say this to the tutor I wanted to tell him that if I put a comma in the wrong place there are professors at universitys who notice it and think about it but I think he would have thought I was mad. Can you blame him?

I am trying to improve my punctuation George. I am taking greater care. I will use capitals at the start of sentences and commas in the right places, where they are needed. Question marks are useful and I don't use them enough. I hope you notice George because I am making an effort and it is all for your benefit.

This week's exercise is to write a poem. I've done one George but Im' not that sure about it. Would you like to read it?

Jack be humble
Jack be meek
Jack decided
Not to speak

I showed it to Buster and he said it was an interesting twist on the nursery rhyme. Well its not just a twist is it George "its the truth". I am not sure about handing it in.

I told you in my last letter about how I tried to tell you that the tape was a fake, But your lot would not believe me. I didn't know what else to do George. I felt guilty. My family are not catholics but me dad did take us to church when we were bairns and granddad was a freemason dad said so I guess there is religion. I did know what I had done was wrong George I knew it was wrong while I was doing it. And then he killed that next lass. I might forget a lot of things but I will always remember her name I read it in the Echo first the headline said Ripper keeps his promise but it wasn't his promise it was mine to you wasn't it She wasn't a prostitute she was a student young lass same age as me.

I thought I'd wished her death I thought I'd made it happen by saying what I said on the tape. Them Dear Boss letters George they're like a kind of spell. Don't get me wrong Im not superstitious like my mam was don't believe them chain letters send this one or else youll get cursed she was always doing them. this is what magic really is Words that can change things. it's just a feeling you get from reading them. Its like they have a power that comes from who wrote them. it was like Id let the genie out of the bottle when I used what he wrote. I was meddling with powers beyond my control.

That's a cliché George I learnt that in class last week and they should be avoided but I reckon they do ther own job. It was like Id done the spell but I was the wrong person to have done it. It wasn't my spell And there was no undoing it once its been cast thats what it seems like to me.

I thought it was Jack that was killing women not anyone else Jack dear boss jack I thought I'd brought him back or summoned his spirit. I could not live with myself George I could not look at myself in the mirror. I drank a lot George in them days just as much as I did before I got locked up in gaol.

Yours faithfully

Jack Sprat

WRITING EXERCISE 2
POEM
By John Samuel Humble

THE RIVER
The river sweats
Oil and tar
The barges drift
With the turning tide
Red sails
Wide
To leeward, swing on the heavy spar.
The barges wash
Drifting logs
Down Wearmouth side
Past Roker Park.

John,

Despite its apparent simplicity, this is a remarkably sophisticated piece of writing. It has a haunting quality that makes
me feel as if I've read it somewhere before . . . which, it
emerges, I have.

I felt it so sophisticated that I plugged the verse into Google.
This showed me in short order that it is extracted from *The
Waste Land*, pretty much the single most significant poem of
the twentieth century. Eureka! You've been cunning enough
to change a couple of words to make it local to you but otherwise it's word for word. I happened to be in the library earlier
today so I checked in with Philip and was not that surprised
to learn that the library has a paperback copy of T.S. Eliot's
Collected Poems and that it is currently on loan to one
Humble, J, Prisoner number 8133.

John, it's not my job to give you a hard time. If you don't
want to write a poem, don't write one. I really won't be
bothered. This course is not a test or a competition, it's a
way of exploring your own abilities to write, stretching your
own imagination and I hope that it will give you some skills
for doing both those things. If you want to write something
different, tell me, I'd love to read it. In fact, write what you
like, but do practice writing, and not copying out, which is
of extremely limited use in this context.

I'll be completely honest; I've saved you from a right going
over by spotting this before the class. Because I tell you now,
Kenneth would certainly have spotted it. There are many
poetry buffs who pretty much know *The Waste Land* off by

heart. If you're going to plagiarise, which I wouldn't recommend, you should aim for more obscure sources.

In all honesty, though, I'd be interested to hear what made you choose *The Waste Land* and what you think of it.

Let's not bother with a mark for this exercise.

Yours,
Martyn

For the past four years a vicious killer has been at large in the North of England. There have been to date 12 horrific murders and four brutal attacks. The evidence suggests that the same man might be responsible for all of them. If so, he has struck 13 times in West Yorkshire, twice in Manchester and once in Lancashire. Large teams of police officers, including Regional Crime Squads, are working full time in West Yorkshire, Sunderland, Manchester and Lancashire to catch him. His original targets were prostitutes but innocent girls have also died. You can help us to end this terror...

HELP US TO CATCH THE RIPPER

Have you seen the handwriting? [if you haven't it's on the back page]

Have you heard the tape? [if you haven't ring the nearest of the following telephone numbers: Sunderland 43146 Leeds 464111 Bradford 57623 Manchester 313130 Newcastle 67541]

Do any of these questions describe someone you know?

- Has a Wearside (Geordie) accent?
- Is physically fit and reasonably strong?
- Travels between, or has connections in, the Yorkshire, Lancashire and Sunderland areas?
- Perhaps shows disgust of low moral standards?
- Is a manual worker or has access to tools?
- Possibly lives alone or with aged parents?
- Is prone to sudden outbursts of emotion?
- Owns a car of his own or has access to one?
- Sometimes stays out late at night?

- BUT DON'T DISCOUNT ANY SUSPICIONS BECAUSE OF THE QUESTIONS. IF YOU HAVE ANY DOUBTS AT ALL, CONTACT THE POLICE AND HELP CATCH THE RIPPER.

IF YOU ARE AN EMPLOYER

- Does your firm possibly have business connections throughout the North of England, especially in the Yorkshire, Lancashire and Sunderland areas.
- Have you an employee who was available in Sunderland to post an envelopes on the following dates:

March 7/8, 1978.
March 12/13, 1978.
March 21/22, 1979.
Shortly before June 18, 1979.

Through his duties or being absent from work was he available to attack the 'Ripper' victims (see centre pages) on:

July 5, 1975	February 6, 1977	December 14, 1977
August 15, 1975	April 24, 1977	January 21, 1978
October 30, 1975	June 25, 1977	January 31, 1978
November 20, 1975	July 10, 1977	May 17, 1978
January 20, 1976	October 1, 1977	April 5, 1979
		September 2, 1979

26 Hawarden Crescent
Sunderland

27th December 2007

Dear John,

Today I visited Francis's grave. He is buried at the crematorium just off Chester Road. It has been fifteen years to the day since he died. I still miss him. Lord alone knows he wasn't a great conversationalist but I think he came from a generally less talkative generation – I am from a slightly later one, my dear, hence my own proclivity towards excessive verbiage.

The crematorium is, perhaps peculiarly, one of my favourite places in town. Oh, I am of course fond of Barnes Park, the formal Victorian grandeur – perhaps even more so than the Winter Gardens, which seems ever so slightly corporate now that it has revamped. Barnes Park has always been a popular park, and by that I mean for the people. Not so the Winter Gardens, which seems to me a little hoity toity. I can remember all too well bands playing on the band stand at Barnes Park – it would happen frequently well into the seventies, when there were still a number of colliery bands about the place. I quite giggle when I recall that fruity, parping sound, much more joyous than the melancholy lament television advertising executives would have us misremember as representative of the North. Perhaps I am being unfair. Perhaps it was always like that in Yorkshire. Not so here!

I digress. The crematorium has remained peaceful. Indeed, the crematorium has remained . . . the crematorium. As all around it the city has changed, becoming at first brightly and optimistically plastic, and then, inevitably, slightly tired and shabby, the crematorium simply persists. It is large enough, for one thing. It protects itself. It is wrapped in its own necropolitical suburbs. One must penetrate the plots laid out for newer arrivals to access the interior.

Francis's grave is simple, as was his service. No fancy headstone, he didn't want one, a plain marker with a trefoil knot engraved on it. Celtic, Victorian funerary ornamentation. Just so. The trinity, infinity and communion. I brought a small hand-tie of daffodils – not that he liked flowers, particularly, but it seems nice to brighten the place up. I like to see flowers on other graves when I visit. I retired to a bench and remembered his funeral. A handful of stoical old men, former employees of the water board. Others of Francis's generation would have had army colleagues, bravely supporting their fallen comrade in a clutch of proudly worn medals, but Francis had a weak heart: he did not serve. The fools who white feathered him did not attend.

As I returned home on the bus, my thoughts turned to you. I recall that your family lived on the Ford estate, not far from the crematorium. And so I write once more. As you can probably now discern, I do so more for my own benefit than for yours. I do not anticipate a response. I simply enjoy writing letters and I have fixed upon you as someone to whom to send them. I really do pray that they offer some small distraction from your quotidian life in prison. I pray also for your wellbeing.

Should you find yourself at a loose end upon your release, please do not hesitate to visit me. Merry Christmas,

Your friend,
Freda

PE8133 HMP Altcourse, Fazakerley, 25th January 2008

George

Had creative writing today and Martyn asked Kenneth to read out his poem to the group. All the lads went quiet and a couple cried. He said it was about some ancient gallic myths. I asked him for a copy and he said it would give him great pleasure but what he's give us is not what he read out to the class. Its obviously just for me George its not what he read. It feels strange I'm not sure what to make of it. No one's ever wrote a poem for me before but I don't think he likes us that much to be honest. Apparently Kenneth is in for manslaughter has another seven year minimum. Martyn thinks he should send his poem to a magazine.

See what you think
Johnny boy

WRITING EXERCISE 2
KENNETH MACPHERSON

Sticks and stones may break my bones
But words will never hurt me
Stanley knives and screwdrivers
Obligatory gerundives
Paring blades and blowtorches
Kernel deconstructions
Scalpel sharps and billy clubs
And pens and swords and truncheons.

Dogs must be carried everywhere
When you play with fire;
Words that scald and garrotte,
Barbed as any wire.

Cut them up, slice and slash,
Put them back together.
You can't.
It won't.
We're scarred and tarred
With pens and swords and feathers.

Of genies and of bottles,
Of demon pacts I sing to you.

The cloth you're cut from,
Pulpy bones,
They're written on and through.

PE8133 HMP Altcourse, Fazakerley, 5th February 2008

Dear George,

George,

Officer,

    We never really knew each other did we me and you you and me. I mean you thought you knew me but you didn't. You never even know who I was even though you did say it was personal. I knew you but it wasn't you was it I saw you on telly read about you in the papers but I didn't know what you do when you go home what your life was like what was it like being George oldfield what you ate for tea what you said to your wife who were your kids what you watched on telly how you thought about things. There was some things you said you were thinking about on telly but was that really it. Im not sure I really know anyone George we say things but what you say isn't what you mean is it. I wish id known you better. Its like when you read a story or watch a film youre in that aren't you. You know how someone thinks then. I don't suppose we will get to know each other much more now. I don't even know Stanley not really I don't know anyone who does. Ive not worn your shoes never mind run a mile in them. I cant watch films now what I used to watch George. Horror and that. The other day I was with buster and we were watching this film murder by decree he says here youll like this john its a Sherlock holmes its got that feller out of Salems Lot the main vampire and Oddball out of kellys heroes it'll be smart this john. I watched it and it was good to start with there was a holmes Ive not seen before and him and Watson were at the theatre and then the prince come in and the crowd at the top in the gods started booing and the ones underneath were cheering and Watson got it back on track. Then the next bit there was this killer and he strangled this woman and you were watching it all from him like it was you like it was your hands and I couldn't watch it I knew it was just actors and cameras but it was like it was my hands George doing devils work my hands with screwdrivers and Stanley knives my hands your hands our hands. I cant think about that George about using your hands like that. You and me George were in it together you and me and him where do you stop where do I begin. I don't know you you don't know me living together in harmony.

I did it because I wanted to do it Nothing more to it than that act in haste regret in leisure me mam used to say.

This morning there was an envelope that had been shoved under my door with some clippings in it. Tom give it to us he said I think this is meant for you john It said cunt on the front. I don't think he knew anything about it It must be one of the guards or if its not it's one of the lads who knows the guards. I feel sick and empty like I did when I first come in george sick to my stomach like a terrible hunger. Its clippings and that from the papers.

Yours faithfully

Humble

I thought I had my feelings under control. But, I was surprised at the amount of anger I felt at John Humble when I saw the news. I thought I had it under control. But I just wanted to flatten him, to smash his face in. If Humble hadn't misdirected the police my daughter might still be alive. I asked myself "why didn't the police take more notice of the women who escaped, who survived being attacked by the real Ripper?" There were not many but they did say their attacker didn't have a Wearside accent. The police should have been more open-minded and taken notice of their descriptions. There is no excuse for not doing that. Why were they so convinced, the powers that be, that Wearside Jack was the killer. I can't understand that.

Q   Are you the author of the letters and the tape-recording posted from Sunderland to the police and the press from a man claiming to be the Ripper?

PS   No I am not. While ever that was going on I felt safe. I'm not a Geordie. I was born at Shipley.

Q   Have you any idea who sent the letters and the tape?

PS   No, it's no one connected with me. I've no idea who sent them.

Text to: 43146
I know who did it George it was me it was a fake it was a hoax tell
him it was a hoax I did it george
Message not sent. Number not recognised.

Text to: 43146
You should have stopped him george
Message not sent. Number not recognised.

Text to: 43146
Its not real george Im not the ripper it was me its tell them it was
not real
Message not sent. Number not recognised.

Text to: 43146
Georgey porgey peter and I killed the girls and made them cry
Message not sent. Number not recognised.

Text to: 43146
That wee lass george that slip of a lass
Message not sent. Number not recognised.

Text to: 43146
Lord forgive me Barbara forgive me
Message not sent. Number not recognised.

Treacle it looks like heavy in the dark thick and gluey sum flows moving slowa than uthas whirls and whorls and swirls and floatas and these let yeh know its really movin fast because these move with the real speed of the rivva thehs a gull just sat theh lettin the curren carry it out tu sea but it cun fly off wheneva it wants not like the wood when that cums down branches with twigs off at angles must uv fallen off trees by the rivva sort uv stuff normally stuck in weahs lots got through and the inky stuff is lush to just watch it flowin through ah rememba timothy hutchinson askin in school whys the town called sunderland and mr Hopkins the teacher says does anyone know and sumwun pipes up is it because it used to be sunny and evrywun laffs at that because its nevva been sunny heah has it its always been wet heah and mr Hopkins says its because of the rivva the rivva Wear it splits the town down the middle it sunders the town splits it asunder its a sundered land the rivvas what its about and the boats and the ships thats why fords called ford because they used to ford the rivva theh me mam telt us there was fellas in boats rivvamen that used tu fish out the bodies at ford because folk wud get washed away if the rivva wuz too heavy and they tried to cross the river like if it had been rainin but sumtimes she said it wusent rain down heah but rain in weardale that would do it so people didnt always know it might rain in sumwheh like Stanhup and thehd be druned people in ford ovah the edge of the bridge theres flows in the treacul and like surges from undaneath ah wunda what's all undaneath the watta if its all fish and are theh lots or is it all crap all mud and silt and chemiculs from north sands maybe beah from vaux and ah climb up on the edge of the barria and the metals cold its like vinega beneath me palms it sets me teeth in edge but ah pull meself up and ah sit in the edge of the barria thehs a few cars going past behind me but no wuns watched us no wuns seen us but when theh lights come from behind ah can see what ah think is me reflection in the watta like flowas uv yeller light behind me head and ah just fall towards it again and again and again and again fallin nevva stops one long fall and ah wake up before or ah hit the watta and ah nevva know which

Fall Man Named

A man who fell from Wearmouth Bridge yesterday has been named as John Humble (23), of Halstead Square, Sunderland. Mr Humble escaped with only minor injuries after plunging 100ft. into the River Wear early yesterday morning.

Dr Peter Rivers
Patient file: John Samuel Humble

10/11/1979

Patient admitted on referral from Sunderland General Hospital
following a suicide attempt. The patient was entirely uncommunicative,
declining to engage in conversation with medical staff or fellow patients,
and had been so at SGH.

Apathetic. Motor activity tardive. Depressed facies.

CBC-Diff (WNL); EKG (WNL); SMA-18 (WNL); Urinalysis (WNL);
Chest X-ray (WNL).

I stressed that the patient could speak when he was ready to do so
and described the routine of the hospital, stressing the supportive
nature of the environment. He has been allocated a room of his own.

Prescribed: 100 mg Benadryl h.s p.o.

11/11/1979

Patient remains uncommunicative during counselling. Depressed facies
as at admission and generally lethargic. Has been sleeping well.

Prescribed: 100 mg Benadryl h.s p.o.

12/11/1979

Patient remains uncommunicative. Given lack of response to questions I
want to try a course of tricyclics.

Prescribed: 75 mg Tofranil.

13/11/1979

Patient remains uncommunicative. Suggest increased dosage of Tofranil.

100 mg Tofranil.

14/11/1979

Patient remained silent for duration of group session, despite antagonism from other patients. Suggest increased dosage of Tofranil.

125 mg Tofranil.

15/11/1979

Attempted structured therapeutic session. Patient invited to sit in the centre of a circle while lead psychiatrist and two additional medical staff seated at the exterior of the circle presented to the patient a series of sensual stimuli. Patient remained unresponsive. Suggest continued medication.

150 mg Tofranil.

16/11/1979

Today the patient presented to my office and said he was ready to talk. I told him how glad I was that he was feeling so much better. He initiated a story about how he had 'slaughtered', in his words, his mother, his sister and his brother. I told him that we knew full well that his mother and sister were alive and that I had been in personal contact with both about his recovery. He waved away my concerns and claimed that he had also been responsible for the murders of five women in London, murders for which he'd never been apprehended. I asked him when he'd committed these crimes. I committed his response directly to paper, so striking was its construction: 'There's the scarlet thread of murder running through the colourless skein of life.' I told him that his answer made no sense and that I was not inclined to believe his outlandish claims. He became uncommunicative once more and was returned to his room.

175 mg Tofranil.

17/11/1979

A breakthrough of kinds after yesterday's shenanigans. The patient submitted to the lead psychiatrist a hand-written note (see attached) explaining his state of mind and requesting immediate discharge. Lead therapist explained requirement to patient to recommence verbal communication before discharge. Suggest overnight observation and discharge pending results.

175 mg Tofranil.

18/11/1979

The patient presented at my office this morning and simply and politely requested discharge. He was disinclined to engage any further in conversation but he had spoken. I felt, on balance, that it would do more harm than good to go back on my word given that he has kept to his side of the stated arrangement. Discharge approved. I have issued him with a prescription to continue his medication with Trofanil at the same dosage and instructions to consult his GP to determine next steps when his prescription expires. A most curious case.

Dear Boss,

I do listen to what you say but I am not ready to talk just yet. You talk about being on the right track and I am. You talk about what I need to do and I think I know. I love my work and want to start again.

This will seem like funny little games but its not. Keep this letter back.

Good Luck. Yours truly

John

PE8133 HMP Altcourse, Fazakerley, 14th March 2008

Dear George,

A couple of lines on page ten of the Echo didn't make much of a splash.

100 foot is a long way George I can tell you. It goes slower than you'd think that fall. Its like the time doesn't move so fast after you've gone off the edge its like its thicker like the water. I had time to think but its daft the things that go through your head I wasn't thinking about water or drowning or anything like that I was thinking about how I should of left a note to Stanley that he could have my records.

Should have walked in off the bank at Ford with stones in my pockets. Some of the papers said Id stones in my pockets after my trial. They like a story don't they George. Some of the papers said Id hit a boat like I couldn't even do myself in without making a mess of it. I didn't hit a boat George that would've been a laugh though that.

When I hit the water I wasn't thinking about anything. the body took over panic or adrenaline or something and it decided for me so I started trying to swim even though I'm not much of a swimmer. It was your lot that saw us and fished us out. It would be wouldn't it. Always on hand when you need them eh George the thin blue line fishing little sprats like me out of the water had they nothing better to do. Didnt slip through the net that time. There was two coppers Id not met either before one of them kept saying are you alright son. There's an ambulance on its way. The other one kept shaking his head. What do you want to do a thing like that for. You've barely lived. You've barely lived. I was just saying Im sorry Im sorry and he was saying its alright don't worry its what we're paid for. And I said no I'm so sorry about the letters. They said don't worry about the letters now and I thought they knew what they were talking about George I thought they knew thought they were forgiving me it was like being born again George like Billy Graham or something dunked in the water and come up something new and here was your lot letting us off. So I kept quiet George and Ive been doing it ever since.

after the fall I was taken to hospital and they kept us in because they were worried about us being at risk. No one understood they couldn't really because I couldn't tell. You can understand that surely George. They still hadn't caught Peter Sutcliffe had they. I couldn't walk into Gill Bridge and say its me whos wrote the letters how about a nice cupper, Can you imagine what would have happened. I would of fallen down the stairs might not have made it through the night. I'd tried to tell them george there was not much else I could do As if the murder of that lass weren't bad enough you had a heart attack but then you know that better than most don't you. no point me telling you that. I felt bad about that too George on top of it all I was responsible for you having a heart attack. I may not of killed you but I didn't help.

Doctors said I was depressed No record of mental health issues in the family but they knew my dad had died when I was just a lad and they knew I didn't have a proper job and they said I was depressed. You might have guessed Id be sent to cherry knowle after what that doris stokes had said Sure enough I was there for a few weeks. Middle of nowhere cherry knowle. Bit like armley gaol on the inside. Big red brick towers and buildings out near ryhope full of nutcases and halfwits. The nurses looked after us though. Bunch of crackers in there George best looking lassies in the country come from sunderland there's not many know that little secret. Between you and me eh.

It was hardest on my mam and it was her I wanted to tell the truth to but I knew that would have hurt her more. She would have been talked about people would have thought it was her fault. "Its always the parents" george. She'd worked hard on her own bringing us up and I couldn't do that to her. I bet you'd think I didn't have the bottle well I had to have some bottle enough to bottle it up.

Yours faithfully

Jack

PE2987 HMP Armley, Leeds, 16/03/2008

Dear Johnny,

How are you doing? What is it like in Altcourse? Are all the scousers giving you a hard time about the football? Remember Johnny we're Sunderland till we die.

I am writing not just to say hello. There has been some news I think you will want to hear. Pest died last Monday. He went through the nets from the threes. No one knows if he jumped or if he was pushed but everyone is telling the same story. The lad was a crackhead and he had a screw loose. Back when I was going out to the Eclipse every weekend this lad Sean lost the plot on too much acid. We used to say he'd gone digital – couldn't speak, like, just nod and shake his head. Pest had gone properly digital, Johnny.

The noise was like a sack of spuds. No shouting till anyone else saw. Pest didn't make a sound on the way down just the nets snapping as he went through. He wasn't dead straightaway. Mr Butler and some of the other guards tried to help him but Mr Butler says it was obvious he was beyond help. He had a broken neck, broken back, fractured skull, the lot. You can't fall three floors onto stone and get away with cuts and scratches. It proves the nets don't work, mind, they're like an elastoplast, just to stop us from whinging on. So much for that.

The guards tried to ease the pain and they gave him some morphine. As you can imagine lots of the lads were jealous about that and there's been people talking of chucking themselves through the nets to get a hit. There's something wrong when people are just thinking about drugs when a lad's died Johnny. Mr Butler's not letting on what Pest said when he was on the floor but one of the lads with a cell nearby says he was whispering mad crap, all that religious Lord and master stuff you heard in the showers that time. Probably making his peace. Pest in peace, eh? Well, he was better at making a mess if you'll excuse the bad taste joke. Anyway I should stop calling him Pest his real name was Renfield. When the notice went up first no one knew who it was about because no one knew his name.

They've been asking us all about the arguments we had with him. They obviously think there's been foul play. I've told them I didn't like the lad and that they wouldn't find many that did but there was no one wanted him dead. I think they believed me. They'll probably read this so I might as well repeat it for the record.

And here's a freebie, in case anyone's reading. There's a rumour that he froze out one of the Paki lads and they've had a hit out on him. But I reckon he jumped Johnny, he was a cracker wasn't he? Seems as likely as not.

Anyway, please write and tell me about life in your new holiday camp. I am thinking that no news is good news but don't forget your old pals here in Leeds. My new cellmate sends his best regards. How's your old pal George? Please pass on my wishes.

Look after yourself marrah,

Richard

PE8133 HMP Altcourse, Fazakerley, 10th April 2008

Oh George,

Your lot didn't catch him did you. You didn't catch him until a year later. People say that was my fault George but I was trying to get you to look harder all along. You really weren't much good were you.

Someone wrote a book about me. Not really about me though was it, It was about Jack. I'm Jack. That's what I said so I suppose it was what I'd wanted. I was so famous people wrote books about me.

You might wonder how that felt but it didn't feel like much. I felt like getting pissed so that's what I did. After a few pints went out and bought a copy. One for the collection a real book in my hands George. They'd stopped playing the tape by then and they'd stopped the phone line so I was yakking on a bit more but not that much. I went up to counter in Woolworths and asked the woman have you got that book about the Yorkshire Ripper. Here I'll have a look. What's it called she said. I stood there for a minute looking at her and she said again whats it called. I wanted to shout out I'm Jack I'm Jack I'm Jack you daft twat. Excuse my language George it was very upsetting and I was drunk.

I said I don't know pet but its got a picture of a tape on the front. There was a lot about them poor lasses more than in the papers all the details. Then there was a whole lot about me or was it about peter Sutcliffe or was it someone else. I don't know who it really was George and they didn't either them what wrote it.

It was strange reading that book. It was schizophrenic. That's a good word that George. thats what it was like because there was all kinds of psychiatrists writing about the murderer and the way hed killed the women and how he was probably an ordinary lad but was in a holy war against prostitutes. I didn't think that was much like me but then I wouldn't would I. Then there was all stuff about the letters which they thought I was probably 42 years old had been in the merchant navy and had lived outside of sunderland that I thought of myself as an avenging angel because I wrote Lord. Well George I didn't see myself in that lot either. Then they said I would probably live in a brick house that was true but doesn't everyone. I went out dressed up on Saturday nights looking for girls maybe I was rejected by them. Maybe my dad went with whores. That was rude that George. I was a loner but wanted to be one of the boys in the pub. I bought girlie magazines and hid them from my mam. When I read that George I chucked all my penthouse over the wall into the crem.

There was one interesting bit George. They wrote that all the books on jack the ripper had been nicked from Sunderland central library. That made me laugh that did. everyone likes reading about that don't they not just me. I only nicked the one from kayll road maybe theres lots more writers like me or maybe theyre just easier to sell. The one thing that they couldn't decide on was whether or not I had clippings well we know I did do that don't we George kept up to date.

There was no rest for the wicked Lord not at all. My voice was still there Still doing the rounds. After the fall I kept my own peace George there was "no other option". Mam and

Stanley and everyone else said I was depressed. I was depressed probably George I was depressed cause your lot couldn't find the ripper I was depressed cause I couldn't find a job and I was depressed cause I felt like crap. I wasn't depressed when I was drinking Ive always liked a drink but I drank a lot then.

Only good thing was no more murders. I started to wonder if hed gone away or if hed topped himself like everyone else I suppose. I started getting on with my life. Did some labouring here and there some odd jobs. Then August 1980 Marguerite Walls. Then November Jaqueline Hills a student in Leeds. Her mam went on the telly Brave woman that George. Why didn't you catch him before he killed that lass. Id done what I could George tried to warn your lot.

After Jaqueline Hills my voice came back again George an echo. new analysis of my voice and Ive got a stammer. I was putting the accent on. Theyve been pursuing lines of inquiry related to that. That was when mr Windsor lewis went on the news to say he thought it was a hoax I was a superhoaxer. Your pal dick didn't like that much George must have felt stupid he said he was 99% certain it was the ripper whod made the tape. He was a good friend to you wasn't he George. Wouldn't change his mind. That wasn't even the end of it. There was a programme the next week with this blind feller on it he was an expert in recording George an expert in hifidelity equipment I bet he doesn't buy his tapes at boots. He said hes certain that theres distortion on the tape that Ive not got a speech impediment That its tape hiss That the batteries were running down Well that might've been true George I didn't change the batteries in Stanleys recorder did I.

Lord it makes me feel crap to think about all that. You might have thought it would of got better when you lot caught peter Sutcliffe but it wasn't all that much of an improvement for me because of what he said. But Ill bet you feel the same about that George I'll just bet you do. The mam of that last lass from Middlesborough I saw her on telly she said I should have those deaths on my conscience. The judge in the trial called us almost inhuman Ive been called some things by judges George. I couldn't do much then could I. Couldn't hand myself in after that. Had to let the dust settle properly not really my fault.

Ta ta George

Jack

TAPE ANALYSIS FOR WEST YORKSHIRE POLICE
Angus MacKenzie c/o Olympic Studios
31/11/1980

The type of tape used has had a considerable effect on the quality of the recording. Notable thuthiness has led to pronounced sibilance of all the 's' sounds and this has perhaps been misread as a speech impediment on the part of the author. Oxide-shedding has produced tape hiss which exaggerates this effect. Cyclic variations in output are evident and most likely derive from the poor manufacturing quality of the cassette used but might also be attributable to a failing power source in the cassette deck used to make the recording. Similarly, considerable print-through and noise degradation have occurred and the levels vary precipitously. There is noticeable wow and flutter and some fluffiness.

In summary, this is all to be expected from a budget C60 cassette produced by EMI for the Boots chain. The recorder used was almost certainly also a budget machine and the combination of the two has proved disastrous for the quality of the recording. Dolby noise reduction would have made little difference given the poor build quality of the apparatus used, but it was not used.

The implications for analysis of the recording are therefore twofold:

1. The suggestions that the author has a lisp may be misguided. The exaggerated sibilance of the 's' sounds may in fact be entirely due to the mechanical shortcomings of medium and machine used.
2. We can at least identify the source of the type of cassette used, if not of the recording deck. Given the distinct regional dialect of the author, it may be possible to limit inquiries to the Sunderland branch of the Boots chain.

PE8133 HMP Altcourse, Fazakerley, 3rd March 2008

Dear George,

The drunk and disorderly that was what did it. The last time I woke up in a cell. Six year ago, Get four cans from fred corners in one of his shit blu bags. Don't work do they handles keep snapping not strong enough to carry cans. Who's carrying the cans not fred corners bags. He won't give us two to bag it up said I should get me own bag a bag for life well I did.

Had some bother with some bairns George. They don't have much respect these days do they. Not like back then when we used to respect our elders. Thats a laugh that isn't it. Maybe you did were always part of the establishment I expect. I did respect me mam she was a fine lady George.

Next thing I knew I was down at Gill Bridge signing these forms and then a copper sticking this big cotton bud in my mouth and wiping it around. thats called a buccal swab that is George its a way of getting DNA from your saliva. I got off with a caution so I was pretty chuffed Didnt think twice about the sample. Didnt give it a second thought, it turns out all this stuff is put on computer. I knew what DNA is got the gist of it anyway. they put your information in this database and youve got a way of finding people from theyre spit or skin. Its like fingerprints but more individual. You can have a look at my DNA profile George. I haven't got a lot but this is all mine all the information what it all comes down to in the end. Wonder what yours was like wonder if it said you had a dodgy ticker. Wonder whats in this for me.

All the very best

The one true Jack

Form MGHA(T)

Witness Statement

(CJ Act 1967, s.9 MC Act 1960, ss. (5A)3a and 5B. MC Rules 1961, r.70)

Statement of: **John Samuel Humble**

Age if under 18: 'over 18' (if over 18 insert 'over 18')

Occupation: Unemployed

This statement (consisting of 3 pages each signed by me) is true to the best of my knowledge and belief and I make it knowing that, if it is tendered in evidence, I shall be liable to prosecution if I have wilfully stated in it anything which I know to be false or do not believe to be true.

Signature:

I'd just come out Fred Corner's shop [a licensed newsagent on the Ford estate]. I'd bought a bottle of cider and was searching in my pocket for cigarettes. I pulled out my cigarettes. I remember that I had just searched in my other pocket for a lighter and pulled out some change and that change had then dropped on to the pavement. I bent down to pick it up and I knocked some of it into the road. I bent down to pick that up and I heard a car coming and I fell over. I leant out for the coins and saw something shining in the gutter. I leant over and picked up a twenty pence piece. I thanked my lucky stars. I put the change in my pocket, pushed myself up and dusted myself off. I checked my bag and I had one bottle of £1.69 In a Star dry cider and it was still intact.

A young man approached me. This lad was thirteen or fourteen years of age. I recognised him from the road on which I live. I think his name is Kane, or perhaps Brent. This lad said: "How mister. Will you get us some bevvy." I replied: "What do you want that for?" The lad said: "Howay, mister." I told him to ask someone else: the lad's only fourteen or fifteen years of age. The young man said: "Howay, you fucking alkie." I replied: "What did you just say, boy?" The young man said: "You heard." I said: "You want to watch yourself, son." He said: "Or what?" I think I then said: "I'll fucking bray you, that's what." I'm not sure if those were the exact words. He said: "I'd like to see you try. You're one of the alkie brothers, you are."

I lost my temper then and I swung my bag at the young man. It struck the side of his head. The bag contained a two-litre bottle of cider. The lad said: "What did you do that for? That fucking knacked." I said: "That'll learn you some manners." The lad called me a "fucking alkie cunt" so I swung my bag again, stepped forward and pushed into him. The lad fell over like a sack of potatoes and then his accomplice shoved me over. I dropped my cigarette on the pavement.

When the young man got up I saw that he had a bleeding nose. The lad called me a "fucking alkie cunt" again. Both the young man and his accomplice threatened me. His friend said to him: "You're bleeding." The young man wiped his nose and looked at the blood and said to me: "My dad is going to fucking kill you, you fucking alkie cunt." I may have told him to "fuck off," I can't really remember. The young man said to his friend: "Howay." I pulled myself up off the ground as the two young men walked away. I said: "That'll learn you."

I didn't touch him. I only swung at him with the bag. It can't have hurt much. I don't think the police should be involved at all. I'll apologise to the lad.

Form MGHA(T)

Witness Statement

(CJ Act 1967, s.9 MC Act 1960, ss. (5A)3a and 5B. MC Rules 1961, r.70)

Statement of: **Andrew Brown**

Age if under 18: 12 (if over 18 insert 'over 18')

Occupation: Student

This statement (consisting of 3 each pages signed by me) is true to the best of my knowledge and belief and I make it knowing that, if it is tendered in evidence, I shall be liable to prosecution if I have wilfully stated in it anything which I know to be false or do not believe to be true.

Signature:

I'd been playing footie on the rec with Brent and we went round Fred Corners to get some pop because we were thirsty. We were just about to go in when one of them smelly brothers comes pushing past us out the shop. I said "Watch out mister" and he swung his bag at us and clobbered us on the head. It fucking knacked. I said "What did you do that for?" and he started swearing and yelling. He wasn't making any sense. He was pissed as anything. I said to Brent just ignore him and then he swung his bag at us again and nearly broke me nose. He fell over into the gutter. He was a sorry sight. I thought I'd better get cleaned up so I went home and told me Da what had happened and he said he had to call the police. I'm not that bothered but you tell him if I see him again I'll kick his head in.

STR Locus	Alleles Called		
D3S1358	16		18
TH01	7		8
D21S11	28		29
D18S51		12	
Penta E	10		13
D5S818	11		12
D13S317	11		12
D7S820	10		11
D16S539	12		13
CSF1PO	10		11
Penta D	8		9
Amelogenin	Male (XY)		
vWA	14		17
D8S1179	12		14
TPOX		8	
FGA	24		25
NOT USED			
NOT USED			
NOT USED			
NOT USED			
NOT USED			
NOT USED			
NOT USED			
NOT USED			

PE8133 HMP Altcourse, Fazakerley, 20th March 2008

Dear George,

Like Ive said you never really have friends in here you never really know the lads here. Its a mistake to think you are friends because something might change at any minute. Its easier for us older ones weve seen enough weve less to prove. But buster is my friend the closest thing to a pal in here. We have our meals together talk about lots of things but sometimes he goes on too much.

Today I went to call for buster round his room and hes sat there on his bed just staring at his hands you know when someones worried about something. I asked what was up I thought it would be something normal like rotas or applications but he says john are you my friend. I said oh aye of course Im your friend man buster but that set a rabbit off straightaway that did. And he said but what sort of friend are you can I trust you. well that depends doesn't it On what On what it is.

Ive got a review coming up its a big one I don't want anyone to know about it of course you don't you might not get it its not that john theres something else my psychiatrist says I should talk about it. The laws not right john all this usual stuff George you hear it a hundred times its not my fault I cant help myself the psyhiatrist says so its because of my childhood. There was this lad John he was no innocent I tell you he knew what he was doing we met in the library we fell in love john and here was me thinking he was a ladies man George I ask you he used to come in the stacks with me sometimes Id find him books he wanted he was sending me all the signals john Im no fool I know when someone wants to and when they don't so I gave him a kiss and before I knew it he was touching me his hands on me john not the other way around honest George I was looking for the door but hed started and I had to listen he changed his mind john told his mother and she went straight to the police they were round like a shot you wouldn't believe the humiliation the trial was shocking aye well I said thats all done now isn't it I do like Buster the thing is John I don't want to go home its got out on my street what Im in for and I cant go back there theyll lynch me I said not to worry just be honest man buster people will understand you don't understand john you cant be what I am where Im from youd be surprised I said people don't really care now do they this lad was eleven john I tried to make him feel better George but thing is hes told us this story about five times now and I'm a bit bored of hearing it its like he doesn't remember. Anyway I suppose I should be grateful he doesn't tell anyone else because if lads in here knew my best friend was a nonce I'd be for it.

Yours

Sherlock Holmes

PE8133 HMP Altcourse, Fazakerley, 24th April 2009

Dear George,

I wonder what my obituaries will be like. I read your obituaries I've always read the papers always been a reader haven't I. You didn't get much in The Times Im afraid George but they did mention me said you were misled and took it personal. Well it was personal wasn't it otherwise I would never have wrote to you personal would I You were the one on the news not anyone else.

The Times was better than the guardian at any rate which was just two lines I thought that was stingy you were all over papers for a while and they didn't mind writing about you then. The Mirror doesn't bother with obituaries. The echo didn't say much I think theyre embarrassed George. It was a good thing you went when you did though wasn't it. You were a bit of a naughty boy weren't you George not that straight with the facts. That poor lass judith ward you took credit for that collar didn't you. All the forensic scientists were working for you George they hid evidence When they let her out they said as much. She wasn't right in the head wanted to get involved in the case what the papers call an attention seeker but that's not the same as being bad is it. I wonder what is worse theyre all fibs and lies and make believe. Whose whopper's the worst?

Do you think I will get an obituary now that I am famous

for being me. Or maybe I will only be mentioned when peter Sutcliffe dies. Before when I was pretending to be him I was in all the papers and on the telly my voice was everywhere. Before when I was being me then I was.

Id got away with it for a long time hadnt I, After they caught Peter Sutcliffe there was still stories about the tapes. They knew then it was a put-on job. After peter Sutcliffe was when I became a hoaxer when wearside jack was born. For a good few year they thought it was a copper with a grudge against you George. That give me the giggles that did Im sorry to say. Your lot were never very good at sticking together were you I suppose its a hard job and people get cross. I bet there were plenty of coppers that did have a grudge against you. There was a couple books I read then one from an FBI agent said hed been in Yorkshire at the time told them my tape was fake straight away. Said the way the lasses had been killed they knew the murderer wouldn't do that. Thing is George peter Sutcliffe did write to the papers he just wasn't as good as me at that.

As long as they thought it was a copper I knew I was safe. Even started thinking I might join the force I knew I was that good at detection if I'd managed to work out how to pull the wool over your eyes. Takes brains that George. Closest I got was security at the pit. A uniform but a mickey mouse one.

There were lots of programmes over the years. I watched them all most of them with Vikki. Sat there in the living room with the bairns upstairs or out and then my voice would come on the telly. I looked George but Vikki never batted an eyelid. There was one called Manhunt, there was another one like that one on jack the ripper part real part acting, They didn't need an actor for me they had my voice. I wondered if I should send them a bill for fees.

There was a big fuss in the echo on the twenty year anniversary it all come back. They had a list of suspects all from town. No one I knew George but you had to feel for them. Theyd done nowt but then I suppose I was the only one knew that. I told everyone down the pub Geoff and them those lads have done nowt the echos barking up the wrong tree, They all just said oh aye Sherlock tell us more. This one journalist from the echo did a couple of books a couple of TV programmes on tyne tees I bought them books George I had to keep an eye on the case didn't I. It was a bit of a worry then sometimes because they thought Id killed these other lasses Joan Harrison in Preston the lass Id mentioned in my letter then this Julie Perigo in Sunderland. That was a worry that I thought they might do us for murder if they caught us. A drink always helped us worry that bit less George you know what I mean.

I suppose that's it. I've finished telling you the truth the whole truth and nothing but the truth. I could give you my whole life story but its not this is your life is it. if it was Im' not sure Id want to meet who theyd bring on. Stanley Vikki Joan Davver Mike Jimmy Mickey Dave Jammer Auntie Eileen Geoff anyone from the Robin. It would be nice if Richard came on and Buster maybe on the TV from gaol. Maybe one day eh George.

I know why it didn't work out with Vikki. She is a decent lass but I was not much of a catch. It was all fine when I'd been working had a job at Nissan but got laid off there had a job as night watchman security at Monkwearmouth Colliery. thats a giggle isn't it. Poacher turned gamekeeper. But they took the piss George didn't let us watch the box frowned on drink. All those nights sat there watching nothing happening on screens just the numbers ticking away in the corner. Just empty carparks and corners of rooms and seats with no bugger in them smoking cigs the only way to pass the time. I jacked it in George it was the nights mainly.

When I wasn't working there was nowt to do but drink I don't always know why I do what I do. Coppers got involved more than once. I couldn't blame her when she packed her bags. Might see the lad when I get out tho he's always been straight with me. Vikki moved away but bill still lives in hylton its where he grew up.

I tried you know George. Set up washing windows Did most work in Castletown and Penshaw would you believe that. I think people liked my voice over there. they must of found it comforting and familiar. Theres not much money in window cleaning though and when people are strapped they just don't bother with the luxuries and folk are always strapped round here. Did bits and bobs of labouring and that. After our mam died it took the wind out of my sails a bit george and then I just got used to signing on. Moved in with stanley after Vikki kicked us out. We liked a drink together George it worked out alright for a few year then the council kicked us out of stanley s place and got us a new one round the corner. We didn't have money for a van so we carted our things round in wheelie bins. Neighbours were canny not the snobby type. You would of seen the photos of the place if you'd been in court. We weren't expecting visitors so we didn't have a chance to tidy. The papers said it was squalid George. I wouldn't of gone that far. Its not much but it was home. Better than gaol. But as you know from my letters I don't have a home to go to.

Had a meeting with shelter advisor couple of week ago and hes put me in touch with local hostels. Theres one in ford so thats where Ill go tomorrow. I've not wrote stanley to tell him it'll be a nice surprise. I've got three hundred and thirty two pound I've earned. I've got the couple of sweatshirts and jeans they give us when I come in on remand a stack of letters I've been wrote and the letters Ive written and a few bits from the course and that's that.

I've no parole officer Im not that bad. I've had a natter with the Jobcentre lad. He doesn't really know what its like George how can he hes only twenty five. Hes helped us set up a bank account at credit union. Ive got a bank card so thats something new, All my benefits are set up to go in there.

they've give me a train ticket to Sunderland. There's a shuttle bus to drop us at leeds central station. I'm looking forward to a proper drink but its a new leaf isn't it. I'm out into the big wide world now and Ive a clean conscience George Ive been punished I've "done my time". Its what I deserved I was a stupid young man now Im a stupid old man but Iv'e got a clean slate. I'm an honest john now George no more tall stories.

It's been nice getting to know you Its only a shame you never wrote back but I suppose you're not the writing type.

Amen,

John

Herald and Post
6th July 1985

George Oldfield, who as Assistant Chief Inspector in the West Yorkshire Police led the hunt for the Yorkshire Ripper, has died at the age of 61 at Pinderfields Hospital in Wakefield following a long illness.

Mr Oldfield was rested from the case as a result of a heart attack in 1979, and retired in 1983 following a second. In private colleagues acknowledged that the stress of leading the inquiry had contributed to Oldfield's illness. He was misled by hoax tapes and letters sent by a man who was never found, and removed from the case in 1980.

Peter Sutcliffe, 37, was arrested the following year and confessed to the murders of 13 women.

Before becoming a policeman in 1947, Oldfield had served in the Royal Navy. He progressed through the ranks of the West Riding CID and was promoted following the investigation into the bombing of a bus on the M62 in 1974, securing the successful conviction of Judith Ward.

Colleagues remembered a hard-working and determined policeman. He leaves behind a wife, Agnes, and two adult children, Michael and Linda.

NATIONAL IDENTIFICATION SERVICE

PUMVS, Room 391, New Scotland Yard, Broadway, London, SW1H 0BG
Facsimile 0207 230 2100/2199
Direct line 0207 230 3530

Notice of name/sex change, from H. M. Prisons

H. M. Prison   Altcourse

Current name of inmate   John Samuel Humble

CRO/PNCID number   D6732

Prison number   52245

**Reason/grounds for name change, please tick,
(delete not applicable)**

Sex change

Religious

Psychological/medical

Compassionate ✓

Marital change

New name ▓▓▓ ▓▓▓ ▓▓▓

Confirmed by deed poll, please tick, (delete not applicable)

Yes / ~~No~~

Form PUMVS 11

Granta Publications, 12 Addison Avenue, London W11 4QR

First published in Great Britain by Granta Books, 2015
This paperback edition published by Granta Books, 2016

A CIP catalogue record for this book is available from the British Library.

1   3   5   7   9   10   8   6   4   2

ISBN 978 1 78378 086 0
eISBN 978 1 78378 085 3

Typeset by Patty Rennie
Printed and bound by CPI Group (UK) Ltd, Croydon, CR0 4YY

www.grantabooks.com

MIX
Paper from
responsible sources
FSC® C020471
www.fsc.org